The Little Blue Boat

AND THE SECRET OF THE BROADS!

The
Little Blue
Boat

AND THE SECRET OF THE BROADS!

PHIL JOHNSON

ILLUSTRATED BY PAUL JACKSON

Matador
9 Priory Business Park,
Wistow Road, Kibworth Beauchamp,
Leicestershire. LE8 0RX
Tel: (+44) 116 279 2299
Fax: (+44) 116 279 2277
Email: books@troubador.co.uk
Web: www.troubador.co.uk/matador

ISBN 978 1780883 700

British Library Cataloguing in Publication Data.
A catalogue record for this book is available from the British Library.

Printed and bound in the UK by TJ International, Padstow, Cornwall
Typeset in 12pt Palatino by Troubador Publishing Ltd, Leicester, UK

Matador is an imprint of Troubador Publishing Ltd

This book is dedicated to my children, Nicola, Alex & Tim; and my best friend, my fantastic, talented, beautiful wife Fi.

I'd like to thank Paul Jackson, artist, sculptor and storyteller; for his brilliant and inspirational illustrations.

Special thanks to Clare Weller, Steve Birtles and Nick Sanderson
at the Broads Authority, who, along with their colleagues and supporters, protect and care for one of the the world's most precious places.

Grateful thanks also to
Nick Crane, Jo & Roger Fredenburgh, Marilyn Brocklehurst,
Paul Nettleton, the "Friday Nighters", Hol and Naomi Crane, Martin Kirby and Andy Bloy for advice and support.

The Broads – "A breathing space for the cure of souls."
Ted Ellis, 1909 – 1986

Illustrations by Paul Jackson, Artist, Sculptor and Storyteller.

Map showing where some of the events in the story take place.

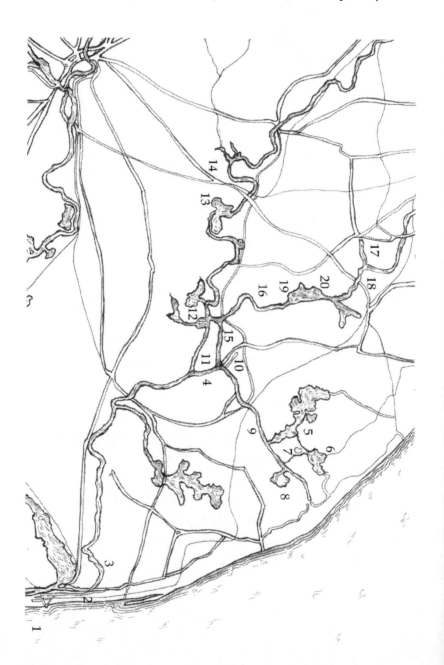

Key:

1 The North Sea – Where "The Little Blue Boat" is rescued by the lifeboat.

2 Gt Yarmouth Yacht Station – Where Pincher Pete first tries to steal "The Little Blue Boat".

3 The River Bure – The night in the reeds with the Swan.

4 Thurne Mill - The Moorhen.

5 Hickling Broad - The Lodge and the Princess.

6 Waxham New Cut - The old mill, the Cranes and the Konik horses.

7 West Somerton Broad - The Pike and the little dog.

8 West Somerton - where The little Blue Boat was stolen by Pincher Pete.

9 Potter Heigham - Bridge where Pincher Pete nearly ramemd a poor cruiser.

10 Womack Water – The Geese attack Pincher Pete!

11 River Thurne – Able Sea Bear, Teddy finds the Swallow-tail butterfly larvae.

12 Ranworth – where bears can fly!

13 Belaugh – where "The Little Blue Boat" rescues the baby Grebes.

14 Coltishall - where the Otters begin their journey home.

15 St Benet's Abbey – dropping off the Bishop.

16 The River Ant – The ancient burrows.

17 Dilham – Where Pincher Pete steals "The Little Blue Boat" again!

18 Wayford Bridge – Where Pincher Pete is arrested (yippee!).

19 Gay's Staithe – Where "The Little Blue Boat" and the Children are reunited.

20 Barton Turf – The boatyard.

But where is "The Secret Broad?"
– it's somewhere on the River Ant, between 16 and
19… but don't tell… it's a secret!

The water is waiting for you. Explore, enjoy, have fun.
Respect the creatures that live there, and remember –
always wear a lifejacket!

CHAPTER ONE

Escape!

"Got any more Marmite sandwiches?" asked the gull.

"No, sorry, you and your gull-friend ate them all last night" said Able Sea Bear, Teddy, "keep quiet though, otherwise they'll hear us!"

"It's alright," said the gull's, gull-friend, "the lifeboat men won't hear or understand us, they're humans, and people don't usually speak bird or animal."

"Or fish, they don't speak fish either," added the gull

nodding. Like most gulls he was a large, white bird with black markings on his wings. Gulls live near the sea and eat small fish, crabs and all sorts of leftovers; in this case, he and his gull-friend liked Marmite sandwiches. They liked them very much.

The Able Sea Bear, Teddy sat back on the old thin cushions just inside the cabin of the tiny yacht. He could just see the bright orange survival suits of the inshore lifeboat men who'd taken *The Little Blue Boat* in tow. The lifeboat men were towing her into Great Yarmouth, a seaside town in Norfolk famous for its golden beaches and piers.

It had been the most worrying and confusing twenty four hours in the small bear's life.

"Yesterday," he said to the gulls, "things were going really well. Rod, he's the lovely man who owns this boat, went for a walk on Southwold Quay."

"That was nice for him," said the gull.

"No it wasn't," replied Teddy, "you see he felt very ill and he collapsed!"

"We know, we saw it," said the gull's, gull-friend. "An ambulance took him away," she added.

"Then," continued Teddy, "that power boat owner, who was moored alongside us, undid his mooring ropes and started his engines, and that loosened our ropes."

"That's why the tide, which was rushing out of Southwold at high speed, carried you out into the North Sea", said the gull, "It's a very good job we spotted your owner's uneaten sandwiches and swooped down to help you…"

"It's also a good job they were Marmite," added the gull's, gull-friend.

"Why is it a good job they were Marmite?" asked Able Sea Bear, Teddy.

"We like Marmite," said the gull, "but we don't like cheese,"

"*Yuk* no, not cheese," added his gull-friend quickly, "we'd have left cheese. See you soon, good luck!" With that the gull and his gull-friend took off and flew away.

The Little Blue Boat and its owner Rod, a retired teacher, and the boat's Able Sea Bear were sailing from Maldon in Essex to the Norfolk and Suffolk Broads when sickness had struck. They'd stopped for a night at the pretty little town of Southwold in Suffolk when Rod, the owner, had been taken ill.

The Little Blue Boat is very small for a yacht, 4.06 metres long, or a little over 13 feet long in granddad measurements. She has a small cabin, just big enough for two grown-ups, and of course room for a teddy bear. She has a set of old sails and an ancient outboard motor, which like many old engines has a mind of its own and will only start when it wants to, despite being grumbled at, shouted at and pleaded with by its owner.

Able Sea Bear, Teddy came from a long line of sea bears. His grandbear had been ship's bear on a liner, and his great uncle was a captain's bear on a submarine.

Teddy checked to make sure the lifeboat men weren't looking, then crept forwards and poked his head out of the small front hatch to see what was going on. They'd been taken under tow by the lifeboat after being reported adrift at sea by a passing fishing boat.

Peering cautiously out of the front hatch, the Able Sea Bear could see they were being taken along the river just inside the entrance to Great Yarmouth. There were some ships moored at the quayside along the way. This is where all sorts of things are loaded and unloaded from boats, and that's how lots of things are brought here and sent off to other countries. Further along the coast is the Port of Felixstowe, where massive container ships bring stuff in and out of the country; everything from toys to food and cars to computers.

Sitting on one of these ships on the side of the River Yare at Great Yarmouth was a cormorant, a large sea bird, dark and menacing. It was hunched up and smirking. "Found adrift were you, *cackle cackle*," said the bird. "If they can't find your owner, you'll be sold at auction or even broken up! Seen it before, seen it before, *cackle cackle*" it smirked.

"Oh no!" said Teddy, "that can't happen!"

"Oh but it can," replied the cormorant, taking off and flying to the next ship along to continue the conversation. "What else will they do with an abandoned boat?"

"But we're not abandoned, we're really, really not!" said teddy anxiously.

"Ah," said the cormorant moving again to keep up with *The Little Blue Boat* which was being towed along, "I've seen it before, I've seen it before, it's sad but true. Unless of course…"

"Unless of course what?" asked teddy.

"Unless of course, Pincher Pete gets you first!"

"Pincher Pete? Pincher Pete?" asked teddy who was getting even more upset and anxious by the minute.

"Pincher Pete will try to steal ANYTHING, especially boats, you watch out for him," said the cormorant which flapped its wide wings and took off, flying out to sea.

Half an hour later, *The Little Blue Boat* with teddy trying to look as small as he could, was safely under Great Yarmouth's Haven Bridge. The bridge marks the border between the inland waterways and the sea, it's what's called the 'Limit of Navigation' and holiday boats on the Broads mustn't go under it as they might get swept out to sea.

The Little Blue Boat had been towed onto the River Bure, which joins up with the River Yare on the inland side of the Haven Bridge. The River Yare is of course where Great Yarmouth gets its name – Yare Mouth.

The Lifeboat men had handed the little yacht over to the Broads Authority Rangers at Yarmouth Yacht Station. The rangers are nice team of friendly, helpful and very knowledgeable people, whose job is to look after the Broads and to help holiday makers and other river users.

The boat was tied up by the rangers who had noted her registration number and checked the address on their computer to trace the owner. All boats that use the Broads need a special licence called a 'toll' which helps to pay to keep the Broads clean, useable and safe. Rod, *The Little Blue Boat's* owner had paid the toll in advance, and The Little Blue Boat had a special sticker on her to show that he'd done so.

Rod planned to give *The Little Blue Boat* to his grandchildren who lived near the Broads. He'd decided he was a bit too old to sail on his own, and his lovely little yacht should be given to a new generation to enjoy. Sadly he was now very ill in hospital and unaware of the plight of his little yacht and its Able Sea Bear.

One of the rangers came out of the building and spoke to his colleague who'd tied up *The little Blue Boat.* "There's no reply from the home phone number," he said. "We'll have to leave her here overnight and try again tomorrow. The air and sea search hasn't found anyone out at sea so it might be the man who was taken to hospital at Southwold, but I'm not sure. I'm told he's unconscious though, so it will be a while before we know."

With that the rangers went off for their tea break. As they did, a shadowy figure lurked in the bushes. He'd been listening. It was Pincher Pete, a small time thief who was always on the lookout for an easy thing to steal. Luckily crime is very rare on the Broads. The rangers and a special police patrol called the 'Broads Beat' keep a close eye on the waterways. Sadly there's always the odd bad person, and this one was called Pincher Pete.

"An abandoned boat," mused Pincher Pete, "I'll have that come darkness, that little outboard's worth a few quid, I can sell that and buy some fags and booze". He laughed to himself, and shrank back into the shadows.

The would-be thief he had been overheard by a little tern, a fast, pretty little bird which has a yellow beak with a black tip. The shingle and sandy beaches near Great Yarmouth are one of their favourite places to live. There are only around 2,000 pairs of Little Terns in the country and they need lots of help from people to survive.

The little tern flew over to *The Little Blue Boat* to warn teddy what she'd heard. "Oh No!" exclaimed teddy, "We've been warned about Pincher Pete. Oh this is awful, the rangers can't find Rod, and now this nasty man wants to steal us. Boat, we must plan our escape!"

"I'll help!" said the little tern. "Look Teddy, the tide will be coming in again in a few hours, just after dark. The tide will be flowing up the river, inland, away from Great Yarmouth, so why not untie yourselves and let the current take you up the river. Where are you hoping to go?"

"Well," replied Teddy," we need to find the owner's grandchildren. There's Lucy who's eleven, Sam who's nine, and Alfie who's seven. I know they like walking at a place beginning with an 'H'".

"Oh" said the Tern, "you might mean Hickling, or Horsey. They are up the river and to the right!"

"Oh thank you, thank you," said Teddy, pleased that a plan was being hatched. The little tern went back to the shingle bank. Teddy and *The Little Blue Boat* waited for nightfall, and so did Pincher Pete.

The rangers went home, the sky darkened and an owl hooted. In the town the bright lights came on and people went out for an evening's fun on the rides at the Pleasure Beach, on the piers and along the Golden Mile, where smells and sounds of candy floss, chips and cheerful laughter often fill the evening air.

There were some other boats tied up at the Yacht Station too. Their crews had either gone into town or were tucked up for an early night. Teddy blackened his forehead with soot from the old outboard engine so he wouldn't be easily seen. He made sure his lifejacket was tied properly, and then scrambled up the metal ladder, higher and higher. The tide was only just coming in and the water was still very low, making the side of the quay very high, especially for a small bear, even an Able Sea Bear like Teddy.

Eventually he was at the top and he quickly undid the rear rope, but not completely. He then realised if he undid that one, the boat's back would start to move and be pushed out by the tide before he could undo the front rope. "Oh!" he said, "now what?"

Luckily the little tern flew back to help. "I'll hold that rope for you teddy," said the small bird .

"Oh thanks, that's kind of you," said the teddy who rushed over to untie the other rope which was holding the front of *The Little Blue Boat*.

"Gotcha!" gruffed a voice. There in the darkness, moving towards them, was the dark shape of a man, a man with bad things on his mind.

"Oh no - it's Pincher Pete!" whispered teddy. The little tern was expecting this and called out a warning, very loudly. Teddy threw himself to the ground holding the front rope and lay still, hoping not to be seen.

As Pincher Pete got nearer he rubbed his hands. "Oh this'll do me nicely, a little boat I can make a few quid on, ha ha." He edged closer and closer to the rope, lowering his body to hide in the growing darkness. Then, just as he was about to grab the ropes, a flock of little terns flew out of the blackening sky and bombed him!

"Hurray!" shouted Teddy, "My very own air force!"

Pecking and diving around him the terns came, one after the other, urged on by their friend holding the rear rope. "Quick Teddy, go, go, go!" shouted the little tern.

Teddy was very lucky, terns don't usually come out at night but tonight they were on a special mission to help him. Teddy finished un-doing the front rope and carefully but quickly climbed back down the ladder into the boat. The little tern threw the other rope onto the boat and said, "Go quick, go quick, let the tide take you, hurry hurry!"

Teddy rushed round and grabbed the tiller to steer the boat away from the other boats tied up next to it, so he could head up the river.

Pincher Pete, his arms waving above his head to fight off the bird attack, said, "Oh no you don't, I'm nicking you!" and rushed toward the quay to get on the boat. He saw how low down the boat was, but his greed got the better of him, he started to climb down the ladder but half way down he jumped… just as the boat moved off.

Pincher Pete had misjudged his jump and a loud splash tore through the night. "Agh drat, come back here, I'll have you yet!" screamed Pincher Pete, who suddenly realised how stupid he'd been. Struggling to get to the ladder that linked the water with the land, he felt very cold. The water soaked into his clothes making them very heavy and dragging him down. Swimming in clothes is dangerous. People in the cruisers tied to the quay heard him shouting for help and came out. They didn't know he'd been trying to steal a boat, otherwise they'd have called the police.

Pincher Pete had forgotten just how cold river water can be, even in the summer and especially at night. If you are cold your muscles don't work as well so it's very hard to swim. Pincher Pete wasn't wearing a lifejacket and could well have drowned if it weren't for the help of holiday-makers, who pulled him onto their hire boat and helped him up a ladder. The thief wasn't grateful though; he cursed under his breath and looked around to see if there was anything he could steal from their boat as well.

The Little Blue Boat and teddy were now heading for Acle Bridge, a few miles from Great Yarmouth up the River Bure. With the mast still down, lying on the deck, they were able to pass safely underneath it, passing the Bridge Pub on their left, or 'port' side in boat language.

"Well done Boat," said Teddy, "let's find a quiet spot in the reeds to stop, we can wedge ourselves in a little dyke to spend the night, I think we both need some sleep."

With that they let the current take them along until the Able Sea Bear spotted a little opening. He pushed the tiller across to turn the boat, the rudder behind them moved and the boat went into the reeds where it came to a stop.

"Do you mind!" said a rather posh voice. It was a large swan which had been sleeping.

"Oh sorry, sorry," said Teddy. "We really didn't mean to wake you."

"Well that's alright, just don't snore. I hate snoring. Let's say hello in the morning. Night night." With that, the graceful swan tucked its head under its wing and went back to sleep.

What a day, thought Teddy as he climbed down into the cabin. *I wonder what tomorrow will bring?*

The moon shone pale, watery of light on the dyke. A dyke is a small ditch or channel and they help drain water from the land into the rivers and Broads.

Back at Great Yarmouth, behind a hedge, Pincher Pete was drying his clothes. "I'll get that boat," he said to himself. Spitting on the ground, he wiped his unshaven, dirty mouth and dripping nose. "I'll have that boat, and that wretched teddy bear, just you see, just you see."

CHAPTER TWO

A Royal Rescue!

The gentle waking sunlight squeezed through the reeds on the banks of the river, brushing the sides of *The Little Blue Boat*. The Able Sea Bear was dozing, as bears tend to do, waiting to see what the day would bring and trying to make a plan. The swan, the large white grumpy swan they'd disturbed the night before, was watching them, his head held high by his strong, slender neck. Swans are one of the largest flying birds; their wingspan, that's the widest point when the wings are stretched out, can be as much as three metres.

"Ah good morning little bear," said the swan softly. "I trust you slept well in my reeds?"

"Oh, hello swan, yes er thank you, um, sorry again for waking you last night, you see we…" but the bear was interrupted by the swan.

"It's not a problem. Now where are you going?" the swan asked.

"Well, we're not quite that sure really, somewhere beginning with a 'hhhh' .

"A 'h'?" repeated the swan

"Yes," said the Able Sea Bear, "H."

"Well, there's Horning, Hunsett Mill, How Hill, Hickling, Horsey Mere," listed the Swan, trying to be helpful.

"And don't forget the Hunter's Fleet base," squawked the little tern, who'd flown from Great Yarmouth where he'd helped the boat and the Able Sea Bear the day before. He just wanted to find out where they were after their dramatic escape; it was the talk of the ternary. Everyone was tweeting it.

"Um, I could try them all," said teddy enthusiastically. "Let's start with Horsey!" he added, and then looked around waiting for someone to take charge and do something. But no one did. The Able Sea Bear *was* in charge, he'd got his first command, he was the skipper, the captain. He was the only one who could navigate *The Little Blue Boat* to safety before she was taken away for being a hazard to navigation by the rangers, or worse, stolen by Pincher Pete.

Time was short, it was the school holidays and the

Able Sea Bear knew if he wanted to find the children he had to do it quickly.

"Right Boat," said teddy in his best captain's voice, "let's cast off!" He had learned that expression listening to Rod, the small yacht's owner, who used to say it before they undid the ropes and left riversides, pontoons or quaysides.

"You aren't cast on!" said the swan, "In fact, very bad seamanship, you spent the whole night *untied*, you didn't secure your vessel to anything, and it was only the reeds that held you tight and safe, not recommended, oh dear no." The swan shook his tall, towering white head with his jet black eyes and orange beak.

"Ah yes, sorry, oh dear, I am supposed to be an Able Sea Bear too", said Teddy, his head bowed in shame.

"Well," said the swan "come along you've got to go, the tide will change very soon and the current will be against you. Is that an outboard motor on the back of the boat there?"

"Yes it is!" exclaimed the Able Sea Bear. He put out his strongest paw and grasped the pull cord. He tugged for all his worth. Nothing. He checked the petrol was switched on so it could flow into the engine and that there was petrol inside the little tank on top of the motor, and then pulled again, and again, and again. There was a cough, a splutter and a big puff of black smoke, and then silence. The outboard was not going to start, well not today anyway.

Teddy scratched his head. Then he remembered. The

owner, Rod, had bought a new little electric outboard motor and a new battery just to use on the Broads. Teddy dived into the cabin and scurried around looking inside the small storage areas under the cushions. "Yes!" he exclaimed coming back into the daylight, dragging the small electric engine. He could barely lift it.

"Allow me," said the swan, who hopped into the cockpit, swooped his majestic head into the cabin entrance and helped pull the small electric outboard motor up and put it in place on the transom. That's the flat bit at the back, or stern of the boat in boat language.

Teddy quickly tightened up the little clamps that stopped it falling off and into the water. He then connected it to the battery, which was inside the boat in a special little plastic box all of its own, and pressed the button. There was no cough, no bangs, just the gentle sound of a slight hum. "Hey Boat, I think we can go!" With that, he put the engine into gear; that means sending power to the propeller which turns through the water and pushes the boat along. Teddy turned the tiller to steer the boat out of the reeds and up the river.

"Keep going then take the right turn in the river, that's the River Thurne, keep going to the very low bridge, go through that and then ask any passing birds, they'll tell you the way from there," smiled the swan who then stretched his wings, flapped them a few times and pushed his head under the water looking for breakfast. Swans like eating weed, tadpoles and insects. You can feed them fresh bread, but not old bread as mould can be poisonous to swans. They are protected by the law, and a swan's nest mustn't be moved or interfered with in any way at all.

Soon a big bend in the river lay ahead, but before they could take the right turn, teddy went cold; he'd seen a ranger in one of their special patrol boats coming towards them. The ranger looked friendly and very nice, and the rangers at the Yacht Station had been so kind, but teddy was frightened. If the rangers found *The Little Blue Boat* with no one but a teddy on board they would surely take it in tow, and who knows what would happen, especially if Rod the owner was still in hospital, or worse.

Teddy suddenly saw a beautiful white windmill, its wooden sails standing proud over the landscape that it towered above. He quickly turned the tiller sharply to the left, which moved the rudder behind the boat and made *The Little Blue Boat* turn to the right (that's how a tiller works, you push it the opposite way to the direction you want to go in, it sounds strange but it's just the way of boats). *The Little Blue Boat* turned into the dyke beside the big white mill, just as the ranger's boat went by. *Phew* thought teddy, *that was a close thing, we may have been spotted so we'd better keep going,* and with that he pushed the tiller right over so the small yacht turned in the entrance of the small stretch of water, passing lots of neatly moored boats, and went back out onto the river to continue their journey.

They were now on the River Thurne.

"Well Boat, that was a lovely windmill," said teddy.

"It's not really a windmill," said a voice from the water.

"Well it looked like one to me," replied the Able Sea Bear. "Who's that? I can't see you."

"I'm a moorhen," said the bird, swimming beside the boat on the surface. "You know a moorhen, we look a bit like coots, but we are more colourful and have red on our beaks. Coots are a bit bigger and have black on their beaks. The easiest way to remember is moorhen – more colour! That's simple isn't it!

I don't like people pointing at me and shouting 'Oh look, it's a Coot' because I'm not, I'm a moorhen. Coots also like to argue, argue all the time. Honestly, try spending half an hour by the side of a pub with a coot and they'll want to argue about anything and everything — the weather, the state of the reeds, the size of swans' eggs, even the decisions of the Bittern Council," said the moorhen.

"The Bittern Council?" queried the Able Sea Bear.

"Oh yes, the wisest and most powerful gathering on the Broads, very important is the Bittern Council. It's the secret gathering run by the bitterns, they're one of the rarest and most secretive birds in the whole country.

That windmill is a wind pump by the way, I should know, I was hatched within sight of it. It is a sort of windmill but it was put there to pump water out of the land and into the river. People think there are lots of windmills on the Broads but most of them are really wind pumps, built to drain the land. Nowadays there are special electric pumps to do that work. Some of the birds would love it all to be damp, boggy marshland, but others like me are very happy with the way it is."

"Where's Horsey?" asked teddy.

"Horsey Mere? Oh, turn left after the low bridge at

the next village along this river called Potter Heigham, it's a very famous bridge as its very, very low. Some boats can never get under it and most have to wait until low tide. You might just squeeze through as your mast is down, and then just ask any passing bird the way to Horsey."

With that, the moorhen swam away. A small boy on a passing cruiser shouted, "Oh look Dad, it's a coot!"

The moorhen shook its head, tut tutting as it went. "Oh no, here we go again," It muttered through a clenched beak.

Potter Heigham Bridge got closer and looked low, very low. Teddy crept behind another small yacht and overheard the people on it saying, "Quick, if we don't get under the bridge soon we'll have to wait hours for the tide." Teddy made sure *The Little Blue Boat* was in the middle of the river, as the middle of Potter Heigham Bridge is its highest part, and they'd have the best chance of getting under it there.

"Ohhh Boat, this is tight, get as low as you can..." Teddy watched the front of the boat go dark as it became covered by a shadow. The front of the boat, the bow, was soon under the old stonework, and the tiny yacht went under the bridge. Potter Heigham Bridge has been there since medieval times and is one of the oldest river bridges around.

They motored gently on, the small electric outboard quietly humming. They passed lots of pretty little wooden holiday homes, some looking like big sheds with windows. Some had people sitting outside waving as they went by, others were closed up and quiet, their owners away. Then after a while the river split, there was a left turn, and a right turn. Teddy steered the boat to the left. The reeds got thicker and soon the river opened out into a big area with lots of little inlets and small gaps between the reeds which looked inviting. Teddy carefully followed the other boats and found they were on the wide, majestic, reed-fringed Hickling Broad.

Teddy tried to keep close to the reeds and as far away from prying eyes as possible so he steered along the shallow side of the Broad.

As the small yacht nosed her way into a tiny dyke, teddy said, "This IS fun! All this beautiful landscape and no one else in this dyke but us and the birds!" But he was mistaken. As he went further down the dyke he saw the thatched roof of a white wooden building. In front of it was a beautiful girl who was crying. *Oh that's very sad,* thought teddy, and slowed the engine down stopping by the edge of the dyke close to the building.

Beside the girl was a small dog, it rushed over to *The Little Blue Boat* barking. "Oh," said the young woman, drying her tears with a small tissue, "come here!" she called to the dog, "Come on quick, it might be another photographer, quick we must go back into the Lodge and hide. She turned and went into the old, pretty building and closed the door.

The dog sat beside the boat growling. Teddy looked it up and down and sniffed the air. The dog then realised teddy was friendly and not a photographer.

It doesn't seem to be a nasty dog, thought Teddy, and then in his best dog voice said, "Er hello I'm Able Sea Bear, Teddy, and this is *The Little Blue Boat*, your owner seems very upset."

"Woof, yes," replied the dog, "she's not just anyone you know; she's a Princess from a small country near Italy. She's come here for a secret holiday to decide whether or not to marry her boyfriend. The trouble is wherever she goes she can't get any peace because a magazine has offered a big reward for any photographer who gets a picture of her, and one has been following her everywhere. Sadly he's found out where she is, and now the poor Princess can't leave this lodge for fear of being photographed. She desperately needs to get to the pub on the other side of the Broad in secret."

"Ah," said Teddy, "we could help if we could take her over to Hickling. The photographer would never think a Princess would travel in a small scruffy boat like this. But how can I tell her we can take her over there?"

Then a shadowy figure moved through the reeds. Teddy shrank back in fear, "On no! It's Pincher Pete!" he said under his breath. A feeling of butterflies rushed through his tummy. Teddy froze, fearing the worst. He went into a massive panic, the sort of panic you get when you've suddenly remembered you haven't brought your homework in. He needn't have worried.

The figure got closer; he was tall, with an old coat and a hat. In his hand was an ancient wooden paddle. It wasn't Pincher Pete.

"Hello teddy, I'm the Marsh Man," said the man softly. "I've been hearing about you and *The Little Blue Boat*, and I've followed your journey too. Don't worry I mean you no harm, I'm here to help where I can."

The Able Sea Bear stuttered and spoke. "You can talk to me and I can talk to you?" he said, very surprised.

"Yes," said the Marsh Man. "I can talk to the animals, the birds and I speak most varieties of fish too. More importantly they can all talk to me." He smiled reassuringly. "You can use that last bit of power in your battery to run your little electric motor and take the Princess to meet her boyfriend," said the Marsh Man. "You can go at dusk. The photographer will never know. I will tell her".

Later, as the sun went down and the birds flew low over the trees heading home to roost, shadows crept across the rippling waters. The dog came out, dragging the Princess by the hem of her dress towards *The Little Blue Boat*.

"What are you doing you silly dog, we're not going for a walk, I've got to go into the car and that horrible man will take lots of pictures and it'll be all over the papers in the morning." She stopped and heard a rustling noise,

"Oh, who are you?" she asked, as a shadowy figure came out of the reeds.

"Hello Princess. I'm the Marsh Man, I'm here to help. I happen to know you want to get to the pub at Hickling. I also know the owner of *The Little Blue Boat* would be happy for you to borrow it. Are you able to steer it across the Broad?"

"Yes I think so," said the Princess, grateful for the opportunity. The dog barked and jumped onto the boat. "It's nearly dark so we should go." The Princess found a life jacket in the cabin and put it on. *That's right,* thought the Able Sea Bear, keeping very still, *even princesses need to wear a life jacket.*

The Princess started the little motor, the Marsh Man pushed the boat away from the bank and the Princess steered it down the dyke into the Broad.

The boat with the Princess and the Able Sea Bear on board moved softly across the calm water, lit by the rising moon. They were soon tied up at Hickling Staithe close to the pub. She headed off to meet her boyfriend.

On the shore on the other side of the lodge, a very bored photographer kept his camera trained on the building's front door. Until he yawned and fell asleep, waiting for his princess, who never came.

CHAPTER THREE

Trapped!

The next day began with a little light drizzle. The soft rain had started falling shortly before dawn, and it woke Able Sea Bear teddy who'd been sleeping in the cockpit - that's the open part of the boat where the crew or people sailing it sit.

Just after the drizzle began, two people crept along the quayside at Hickling and climbed on board *The Little Blue Boat*. It was the Princess and her future husband.

"We must get this little boat back," said the Princess, sitting down and grabbing the tiller.

"Of course," whispered her boyfriend, untying first the front and then the rear ropes, which had safely held the small yacht against the wooden quay all night.

"Is there enough power left in the battery for the electric motor?" he asked.

"Let's try, I don't want to use that awful, old oily outboard, the electric one is so much better," replied the Princess and switched it on. "Oh it's very low," she said, breathing in sharply, "Ah but there is...," she paused, starring into the cabin, "Yes, there is a pair of paddles, so we could row aback if we have to."

"Ok, let's go then," said her boyfriend, and with that they pushed off and turned the boat around, the little electric outboard moving them gently into the brightening morning.

The drizzle dried up and a cool watery sun squeezed through the thinning cloud. The boyfriend had found a small, flexible solar panel in the cabin, and, to help charge up the battery for the motor, he'd tied it onto the roof of the cabin and plugged it into the battery.

The lovers sat together on *The Little Blue Boat*. They talked, they made plans and they shared the short but memorable journey. They were together and alone, except of course, for a small sea bear.

Soon they came alongside the bank near the Lodge, its white paint looking grey in the early light. The couple got out. "Oh I must leave the owner of the boat a present to say thank you," said the Princess, who went into a small shed next to the Lodge. She held up a wooden boat hook and, taking a garden knife from the shed she carved a note along the middle of it. It read, *With thanks, from the Princess*.

"There," she said putting it inside the cabin, "I can soon get the Lodge a replacement." With that, the Princess and her future husband walked into the Lodge hand in hand.

Well that was a nice thing to do, thought teddy, *we didn't have a boat hook did we boat. Oh, now why didn't I notice that solar panel before? Luckily that nice young man has plugged it in so the battery can be recharged when the sun comes out. Let's go boat."* With that, the Able Sea Bear crept over to the side of the boat to undo the front rope. He then stopped dead still and let out a short sharp squeak.

There, towering above the front of *The Little Blue Boat* was a figure. Luckily it was the Marsh Man. The Able Sea Bear smiled.

"Let me help you," said the Marsh Man, "I'll untie you and turn you round, you need to go to Horsey next, that's down a small turning on your left as you leave this Broad. You ought to raise your mast and get those sails up because that battery is almost out of power and needs time for that solar panel to charge it when the sun comes out. Here, let me help."

With that, the Marsh Man raised *The Little Blue Boat's* short mast and connected the boom, that's the bit of wood which goes at the bottom of the mast and above the cockpit to hold the main sail straight. "Come on Skipper Able Sea Bear, raise your sails whilst you're facing the direction the wind is coming from, or as they say in boat language, while you are 'head to wind'. That's it, pull the sails up and then I'll help you go." Teddy pulled up the main sail, tied off the main sail halyard - that's the rope that pulls it up - and then pulled up the jib sail - that's the front sail in boat language.

"Ready about!" said the Able Sea Bear in his best sailor's voice. The Marsh Man pushed the front of the boat away from the bank, as teddy pulled the tiller towards him. The gentle wind filled the sails and the bow of the boat headed out into the centre of the dyke.

"I know we'll meet again soon. I must go as I need to help the Princess too. We can't have this quiet place over run with paparazzi." smiled the Marsh Man.

"Pappa who?" asked the Able Sea Bear.

"Over keen photographers, who are trying to grab pictures of celebrities when they want a bit of peace. Everyone's entitled to a bit of peace," he replied as he walked away.

As the small yacht sailed away, the Marsh Man went onto the track in front of the Lodge. He woke the sleeping photographer, "Morning," he said,

"Oh hello," yawned the photographer, "Er you haven't seen a young woman leave the Lodge have you?"

"Well yes," said the Marsh Man seizing the opportunity to get the photographer away from the happy couple. "Yes, I think she went off on a bicycle first thing, she said something about going to meet her new bodyguards."

"B - b - bodyguards?" stuttered the photographer.

"Yes, bodyguards," smiled the Marsh Man, "I hear one of them is an ex-boxing champion, and the other used to be a Royal Marine Commando, an unarmed combat instructor. She's asked them to come and find some photographer who she says is stalking her."

The photographer grabbed his bag, his camera and his tripod and started running, running very fast. He ran and ran like he was practising for the Olympics until he got to his car, which was parked along the track. He got in, closed the car door, started the motor and was never seen again. Some say he drove all the way to Scotland and started a new life as a wedding photographer.

The Marsh Man smiled and walked into the reeds. As he disappeared from view, the door to the Lodge opened and out walked the Princess and her boyfriend, "Well the photographer seems to have gone, thank goodness," she said, "what a lovely place this is." They walked off hand in hand, down the track.

An Otter poked her head up out of the water and smiled: "I love happy endings," she said and went back to her fishing.

The Little Blue Boat was gaining speed as it left the dyke and went into the main Broad. "Wow this IS fun," smiled the Able Sea Bear. The wind picked up and the small yacht went fast enough to make a little wave, pushing her way through the water. Then she suddenly slowed down. "Oh no," said Teddy.

"Don't worry," said the otter, swimming alongside,

"It's the weed," she burbled with her mouth half in and half out of the water.

"Weed?" asked the Bear, tugging at the tiller.

"Yes it's special weed," said the Otter. "It's cut in the middle of the channel but allowed to grow elsewhere on the Broad. It's one of the only places this weed does grow and it's protected. Lots of insects, bugs and other tiny things need it, so it must have its space. That's what the Broads are like, lots of special places for lots of special things. Look, you've slowed down because you've got the weed tangled around your rudder, I'll pull it off for you." And with that she dived under the water, her back arching as she did, water running off her soft close cropped, waterproof fur.

Within minutes the rudder was cleared of weed and *The Little Blue Boat* picked up speed again, thanks to the otter.

"Thank you very much," shouted the Able Sea Bear, who was really enjoying himself, and using all the special nautical words he knew. "Steady as she goes, Lee Ho, Amidships, anchors aweigh!" But when a heron flew by shaking its head and *tut tutting*, he felt very silly and sat quietly in the cockpit holding the tiller. "I'm a teddy bear on the Broads not an Olympic medallist winning a race," he said to himself. The boat just carried on, happy to be sailing.

Soon the Boat and the Able Sea Bear had travelled along the stretch of river that connects Hickling Broad and Horsey Mere, which is known as Meadow Dyke. They got to the end and sailed into Horsey

Mere. "Oh more open water, that's great," smiled the Able Sea Bear. Birds of all shapes and sizes flew over them and others waded around the edges of the Broad.

The Able Sea Bear steered the small yacht across the water and up a small channel known as the New Waxham Cut. I wonder if the children might be up here? he thought.

The New Waxham Cut wasn't really that new, in fact it had been dug out hundreds of years ago, but many names on the Broads seem timeless.

The channel was surrounded by trees which gave way to reeds on both sides of the narrow canal. *The Little Blue Boat* continued along the narrow stretch of water. The wind was coming from the west, which filled the small yacht's sails nicely and she was carried quietly along.

The sound of the wind in the reeds filled Teddy's ears. Soon an old mill came into view. The Able Sea Bear decided to stop here as he heard voices and saw people on a footpath on the side of the channel, *perhaps the children might be there?* Teddy thought. He turned the boat so it was blocking the channel, with its nose - its bow - into the reeds. The sails flapped as they were no longer in line with the wind, and were being blown from side to side. Teddy untied the main halyard and quickly pulled the main sail down. He then let the jib halyard go free as well, and pulled the small front sail down too. Then, finding a clump of strong reeds and some wood sticking out of the bank, he tied the mooring ropes so the boat was held firmly to the land, pointing back the way they'd come.

He sat back, time passed, but there was no sign of any children. The boat and the Able Sea Bear were sad. As evening approached Teddy noticed a pair of large birds, flying over and then landing by the old Mill.

"Hello!" he called out, "Sorry if I'm in your mooring. Are you heron's?" he asked.

"Nooooo," said the first bird, rubbing its feathers in mud, "we're cranes, common cranes, bigger than herons and, if I may say so, prettier too!"

"Well," added the second bird, "were not actually *that* common either, there are hardly any of us about these parts, most of our friends and family live in Eastern Europe and Scandinavia."

"We also have beautiful feathers and very long legs, haven't you noticed?" asked the first bird, proudly admiring its knees.

"We like it here, it's peaceful you know," said the second bird. "You're not in our mooring, or rather where we sleep, that's by another mill, called Stubbs Mill just over Hickling way. Did you hear about the Princess?"

"Oh what's happened?" asked Teddy.

"Well," said the second crane, looking around to make sure no one else could hear, not that there was anyone else to hear, except the insects and they were far too busy, "it's the buzz of the Broads" continued the crane, "the Terns are tweeting it; she's announced her engagement and is flying back to central

Europe tonight, apparently she said she was given a lift in *The Little Blue Boat* and is very grateful to its owner."

"That's very nice," said Teddy. "Why did you stop to see us?" he asked.

"The Marsh Man asked us to drop in on you with a warning. There's a bit of a wind coming in tonight, it's swinging round to the north then the north east, so you'll be quite exposed here. It won't be as bad as it has been in the past though, our ancestors told tales of whole villages being swamped by the sea, people being drowned and houses washed away."

"Oh no!" said the Able Sea Bear.

"Yes," said the second crane, "you see this is very low lying, the sea level is the same or even higher than

the land in places, and it's only the sand dunes, the shingle banks and some rocks the people put there, which stops all this area from being flooded. If the sea ever broke through it could go inland for quite a few miles."

"Yes," added the first bird, "some of the waders might prefer that, but really it's best to try and protect this land, for the sake of the insects and animals that live here, and the people of course. Some of us think the people have brought a lot of this flooding on themselves. Anyway, we thought we'd tell you, and one of the bitterns also told us to watch out for you".

"Oh?" said Teddy

"Oh indeed," replied the first bird. "Your journey is being noticed. Not much happens in these parts without the bitterns knowing. I think they like you. Take care." With that they prepared to fly off.

"Are you ready to go dear?" said one crane to the other.

"Yes yes, just let me shake this mud off my leg, can't be seen flying with muddy legs, that would be too common, and we're not 'common' Cranes after all".

After a bit of leg shaking the 'not very' common cranes, flew off.

Teddy undid the ropes and picked up a paddle from the cabin. "Come on boat, let's head back and go into the dense reeds, we'll be safer there." He paddled the small yacht along the narrow cut until the reeds surrounded them again, then he tucked the boat into a small opening and tied her up as best he could. The wind picked up as he tied the mainsail tightly around the boom to make sure it couldn't blow about, and then he tied the loose jib sail tightly around the forestay - that's the metal wire which holds the mast up at the front of the boat.

As the wind blew and the boat rocked with the bending reeds, Teddy shut himself inside the tiny cabin, crawled under Rod the owner's favourite rug and quickly fell asleep.

It was a sleep that didn't last long. There was a crack and a crash. The Able Sea Bear opened the wash boards - those are the cabin's doors in boat language -and he saw that a branch from a small tree had broken off and landed between them and the open channel. They were unable to move and stuck in the reeds with no means of escape back to Horsey Mere. Teddy knew he could never move that branch, nor could the otter, the swan or their friend the little tern. What if the storm came, or if Pincher Pete found them? Teddy was very worried. "Boat," he said, "we're trapped!" Outside things moved in the reeds. Big things.

CHAPTER FOUR

Stolen!

As the grey light of dawn crept softly over the landscape, chilled by the summer night, the small bear felt very alone. "Oh Boat," he sighed, "how are we going to get out of this mess now?"

He heard a rustle in the reeds, then another, he was suddenly scared. Very, very, scared. "Nowhere to hide, nowhere to hide!" he said to the boat.

Then the two, 'not very common' common cranes they'd met the night before waded out of the dimness and hopped up onto the deck. "Morning, morning," they said together, "we've brought some friends, don't be alarmed they are a bit big compared to you," said the first crane.

"Oh, very big compared to you," said the second bird.

Teddy looked up as five large heads poked through the reeds. From the heads came breath, breath which looked like rising fog. "Horses!" exclaimed the Able Sea Bear. The boat rocked. There were five horses, short, light brownish in colour, with broad bodies, large heads and steady, sturdy legs.

One of them nuzzled Teddy, his large nose gently

touching the frightened Able Sea Bear's arm. "Don't worry little friend," said the horse calmly, "we'll help you. You need strong animals like us to pull this branch away for you".

"Won't your owners mind?" asked Teddy in a shaky voice.

"We live in the Norfolk Wildlife Trust's Nature Reserve here at Hickling. We're a type of horse called Koniks. Our family comes from Eastern Europe. We're used to harsh winters and our job here is to help keep the undergrowth under control by eating it!"

"Not a bad job," said another horse, nodding its head. "Eating it is the most natural way of controlling the undergrowth."

"Better than many jobs horses have to do," said a third horse in agreement.

"Right," said the leader, "let's get going then." With that, the horses, working as a team, put their front legs into the shallow water, and, with their strong heads they pushed, and pushed again, slowly moving the branch into the reeds and out of the way, freeing *The Little Blue Boat.*

"Oh thank you, thank you," said the Able Sea Bear, delighted to be able to move again.

"Our pleasure, you ought to try Horsey Mere Staithe, there's a wind pump there and a little shop which sells tea and ice creams, you might find the grandchildren there," said one of the horses.

"That's a good plan," replied Teddy, "it's on the left, sorry, the Port side as we go back, isn't it?"

The horses neighed their goodbyes and went back into the reeds. The cranes flew off into the morning sky, still trying to decide which one of them was the least common, and the Able Sea Bear hoisted the main sail then the jib sail, and turned the boat so the wind would fill the sails and take her down the channel.

Soon they were into the open space of Horsey Mere, heading for the Horsey Staithe, which is the name for the local quay, where they could tie up. There were quite a few boats there of all types: sailing cruisers, sailing dinghies, small motor cruisers and large motor cruisers.

The Able Sea Bear had dropped the sails just before they entered the little waterway that led to the quayside, and started the small electric outboard motor, its battery now charged with energy from the sun after two days of sunshine going into the solar panel on top of the boat's cabin roof.

It was a glorious sight: happy children climbing the steps of the old wind pump, people drinking cold drinks and hot cups of tea at the little café by the wind pump, boaters, walkers and other visitors enjoying the atmosphere. Sadly none of them were the children the Able Sea Bear was looking for.

With sadness in his fluffy heart, Teddy sighed and pulled the tiller towards him to make the boat turn sharply round and they headed back, off across Horsey Mere back towards Meadow Dyke and the River Thurne.

The sun shone down on *The Little Blue Boat* and Able

Sea Bear Teddy as they motored along. After a while they turned to the left to go further along the River Thurne to see if the children might be at West Somerton. Teddy managed to sail some of the way and save the battery, and soon they found themselves in Martham Broad. This is a protected area, you can pass through the middle of the Broad on the way to the small village of West Somerton, but you mustn't go either side of the channel because of the wildlife. It's also very shallow and not suitable for most boats.

Teddy stopped *The Little Blue Boat* on a soft muddy bottomed section of river bank just around a corner. He wanted to put the sails down as the wind had dropped. As he did, he noticed a man fishing on a small chair a few metres away. The man hadn't seen them arrive or Teddy putting away the sails. Next to the fisherman was a small black dog, which bounded over to *The Little Blue Boat* sniffing and wagging its tail. "Oh don't come aboard, please little dog," said the Able Sea Bear.

"No, I won't," replied the dog with a friendly wag. "It's just a bit boring spending all day sitting still while he fishes, you know. I just wanted to say hello."

"Well it's nice to see you, we like well-behaved dogs, it's the ones whose owners let them off their leads to chase birds and animals and upset other people that are the problem," said Teddy, shaking his head.

"Yes I know," replied the little dog, wagging its tail even harder, "I couldn't agree more."

"What's your owner fishing for?" asked Teddy, sitting back in the cockpit, resting his paw on the tiller.

"Pike," replied the dog.

"Pike?" said the Bear, quizzically.

"Yes, they are the biggest and most fearsome fish in the Broads. But…" paused the dog, "they are quite clever, they eat other fish, but always go for the oldest or sickest first, leaving the healthy younger ones to grow and have babies. There's no point in eating all your food supply in one go is there? If you did then you would run out of food. That's a good job really because they are easily the biggest fish around here. They can grow more than a metre long and weigh up to 25 kilograms."

"Gosh," said the Able Sea Bear gulping, "I don't think I want to meet one of those!"

"Don't worry," said the dog, sniffing the sides of *The Little Blue Boat*. "They're scared of people, especially ones with fishing rods! If my owner does catch one he'll weigh it and then put it back straight away."

A boat went by, a flat boat full of reeds lying flat in

neat rows. A friendly man at the helm of the boat waved at them.

"Ah," said the dog, "he's a reed cutter."

"Why does he cut the reeds?" asked Teddy watching the boat disappear around the bend in the river.

"The reed cutters harvest them to use for thatching the roofs of houses, you know those old houses that look like they have hairy roofs? Well they need re-roofing every so often. Almost everyone used to use reeds and straw to keep their homes dry before roof tiles were invented. Reed is used for lots of things: burning as bio fuel, putting into animal feed and even for making paper with." The dog stopped and sniffed. "Mmm, I can smell a rather unpleasant smell, has Pincher Pete been near your boat?"

"He tried to steal it once," said Teddy.

"He'll be back then," nodded the dog, "I've smelt him around these parts recently too. You be careful now, Pincher Pete is not a nice man. Not a nice man at all." With that, the small dog bounded back to be at its owner's side, patiently sitting in the sun waiting for a pike to eat his bait.

Below the water a rather elderly, wise pike sat watching the fisherman. *Does he really think that I don't know he's trying to catch me,* said the Pike to himself. *I know he's got bait on a hook and he's hoping I'll bite it, but I'm not that daft.* The pike just sat, motionless, watching the fisherman from his hideaway under the clear, calm, wonderfully clean water of Martham Broad. The fisherman would have another unsuccessful day, but at least he was in the fresh air with his dog, in a wonderful place.

The Able Sea Bear started the motor and the small yacht gently cruised up to West Somerton. Here the river just stopped. There were a couple of houses and a few local boats tied up. It was quiet and peaceful. There was no one around.

The peace didn't last long. It was suddenly broken and the air became tense. A man with an old fleece walked along the path by the riverside, wiping his running nose on his sleeve. *Urg* thought Teddy, *how horrible*. Then the worst thing that could happen, did happen. The man in the dirty fleece was Pincher Pete. He saw *The Little Blue Boat*, snarled, and then spat in the river.

"GOTTCHA!" he laughed and jumped in the boat. Teddy froze. "Still empty then," said the thief looking around, "a few things to nick in here," he smiled and rubbed his stubbly chin. "This engine will fetch a few quid on the internet and that boat hook. Mmmmm." He stared at the neat little electric outboard motor. "This heap of junk won't go very fast. I like going fast and I like noisy engines, I hate this peace and quiet, it's awful." The thief then spotted the old outboard motor close to the new electric one. "Ah great! A proper engine!"

Oh no! thought Teddy, keeping very still, *that engine is old, noisy, dirty and pollutes the water and the air, that's why Rod bought the new little electric one*".

Pincher Pete stroked the old outboard. He fiddled

with it and banged it a few times with his fist, then pulled the starting cord and the old engine coughed, spluttered and burst into life. "Need some more fuel, ah I'll bet there's some on that boat over there." The evil thief got out of the small yacht and walked over to a nice pretty little motor boat tied up to the West Somerton Staithe. He ripped open a back locker, breaking the lid in the process, and pulled out a plastic 5 litre petrol container.

Returning to *The Little Blue Boat,* he filled the small tank on top of the outboard motor, then lowered the mast. "Don't need this, I need to get under Potter Heigham Bridge before dark and get this boat out of the water. I can strip it out, take everything off it and then dump it, or burn it."

Teddy would have cried, if bears could cry. He was horrified and felt sick to his tummy. The Little Blue Boat shuddered and shook. The motor was revved up over and over again. It spurted into life and thick, oily black smoke spluttered out of it. Big blobs of oil dropped onto the surface of the lovely clean river water and the fish that had been swimming under *The Little Blue Boat* hurriedly swam away in all directions, desperate not to be coated in oil.

Pincher Pete turned the tiller and put the engine into full power and the small yacht went off, far too fast for comfort or safety, down the channel, back the way they'd come.

As they passed the fisherman, the little dog barked fiercely and the fisherman shouted "Oi, please slowdown!"

"Don't care at all," laughed Pincher Pete, who made a rude gesture at the poor fisherman. Teddy wished the rangers were here, or the Marsh Man, they'd know what to do.

The Little Blue Boat quickly became a pest. Rushing along, passing other boats, making them rock, sending a big wash onto the banks. With the mast down, the evil thief headed straight for the middle of Potter Heigham Bridge, not bothering to slow down or check if it was clear with no one coming the other way.

Sadly there was a nice new holiday cruiser with a young family on board coming the other way. It was being taken under the bridge by the Bridge Pilot, whose job was to help boats go under the bridge because it was so low. The cruiser hooted.

Pincher Pete just laughed and carried on. The clever pilot had enough experience and skill to narrowly avoid a serious accident. He had to put the boat's engine into full power in reverse and turn sharply. The holiday boat turned and its bow just glanced off the ancient brickwork of the bridge as *The Little Blue Boat* went through in front of it.

The pilot shook his fist, but Pincher Pete laughed and carried on. *Ohhhh* thought Teddy not daring to speak out loud. *That's just so awful, that poor boat and those poor people, I hope they don't think we always behave like that.*

Soon they were in a wide stretch of the River Thurne away from the village of Potter Heigham. Pincher Pete smiled and then saw the small bear. "That's worth nothing," he said, picking up the Able Sea Bear, "I'll throw it overboard as soon as there's no one looking." Teddy was very, very sacred. More scared than he'd ever been in his life. The small yacht was shaking with worry, the old outboard was rattling fit to burst. It was running flat out, it was hot and it was not at all happy. Pincher Pete held Teddy firmly in his dirty, smelly hands, just waiting for a few boats to pass so he could hurl him into the water. Teddy felt alone, in trouble and without any friends to help him. He found out that he could actually cry after all, and he did.

CHAPTER FIVE

The Flying Bear!

Pincher Pete was about to throw the poor Able Sea Bear into the river, which was very wrong for two reasons. Firstly, it's very unfair on the bear and secondly, it's very unfair on the river and everything that lives in, on or around it. Just as the evil thief Pincher Pete was about to fling the small bear into the river he saw his worst nightmare: a ranger in his launch heading his way.

"Blast those busy bodies," shouted Pincher Pete, "I must get away." He saw his chance, the turning to Womack Water came into view on his right side, or starboard in boat language.

Pincher Pete turned the tiller and *The Little Blue Boat* went down the cut towards Womack Water and the village of Ludham. Then Pincher Pete saw something else blocking his path. "OH NO!" said the thief, dropping Teddy onto the cockpit floor. Coming towards him was not one, not two but a whole fleet of old sailing boats. "EEEK!" shouted Pincher Pete, turning down the engine quickly, "It's the Hunter Fleet coming out of their base!"

The Hunter Fleet are the grand old ladies of the Broads. A beautiful fleet of around thirty boats, all built in the 1930's by a clever boat builder. They were so well made that they are still doing today what they were designed to do all those years ago. Their names are legendary and their graceful lines and classic shapes are admired wherever they go. They have lots of friends and lots of fans and must always be treated with great respect. They also have no engines, so the people on them can only go where the wind takes them, unless they are using a long wooden pole, called a quant pole, to push the boats along with.

The sight of the approaching fleet forced Pincher Pete to slow down. He knew he had to let them pass as he was seriously outnumbered. The Hunter Fleet had lots of friends, far more than him; in fact most of his friends were in prison anyway.

He slowed the motor right down, which was a good job as it was just about to give up and die, it had never been run as fast before. He squeezed passed on the edge of the river, growling as he went. "Ugh," he said under his breath, "ancient sailing boats, old and slow, not for me".

As the last of the Hunter Fleet boats went by, Pincher Pete increased the speed of the motor again and *The Little Blue Boat* sped up, then, the engine gave up. With a bang and a cough it stalled and stopped.

"Blast! Oh blast that old heap of junk!" cried Pincher Pete. "I'll have to steal another motor now." But he was about to have another problem. The boat carried on, only slowing down a little as it approached Womack Island. The thief turned the tiller and went round to the left side of the tree, covered island and as he did, there waiting for him was a reception committee.

Of all the birds and animals that live here perhaps the grumpiest, nosiest, and most argumentative of them all are the geese. They go around mob handed, a big gang of them. They are very happy to live and let live and mind their own business, unless of course they are cross. These geese were the crossest they could be. The birds had all been tweeting, that's without a mobile phone or computer in sight - they don't need them, birds have been tweeting for centuries.

They'd passed the message that Pincher Pete had stolen *The Little Blue Boat* and Teddy. The geese were not happy. Oh no, they were definitely not happy at all. They'd delayed having their dinner to gather and form The Goose Gang to help stop the thief. Pincher Pete found himself right in the middle of them.

"We're the Goose Gang," squawked the meanest, biggest and dirtiest goose, "and we've not had our dinner."

"Wretched birds," said the thief, "I wish I had my shot gun." That was it. The geese reared up on their legs and took off in flights, squadron after squadron, up and over *The Little Blue Boat*. Soon Pincher Pete was trying to protect his head with his arms, as wings, legs and beaks rained down on him. The noise was awful. Teddy watched from the cockpit floor and said to himself, "Is that noisy enough for you Pincher Pete?!"

"Go away you horrible things, go away!" blurted out Pincher Pete, but he was about to get wet. Very, very wet. The Goose Gang forced him to the side of the boat and then over the edge and into the waiting water. *Splash!* He was soon flaying his arms about and trying to get to the shore. Each time he got out of the water the geese chased him back into it again, right up to his waist, forcing him to duck his head under the water to escape their angry beaks.

"At least he's having a hair wash," mused Teddy, "the first time in many a month by the look of it!" he smiled.

The birds landed back onto the water and went quiet. They'd done their work. Teddy crept back into the cockpit and turned on the electric motor. As the birds distracted the rather wet Pincher Pete, Teddy slowly motored *The Little Blue Boat* back towards the River Thurne.

"Oh no!" said Pincher Pete, "That boat has got away again. How? How can it go on its own? And I'm all wet, and oh NO! I've just realised I'm on an island and will have to get even wetter getting to the shore. Oh blast you horrid birds."

The geese laughed and took off.

Just when Pincher Pete thought it couldn't get much worse, it did. Two of the fattest geese flew very close and decide it was time to have a poo, right on Pincher Pete's head. *Splat, splat!*

Teddy and the boat soon re-joined the main river, the Thurne, and then found themselves back on the River Bure, the river where their adventure on the Broads had started, where it meets the sea by Great Yarmouth.

Teddy suddenly noticed lots of bits of greenery stuck in the shrouds - those are the wires that hold a mast up in boat language. The mast was down but the shrouds were hanging loose, bundled up and they'd caught bits of plants as they rushed passed at breakneck speed when the boat had been stolen. One of those bits of plants had something interesting on it, "little larvae", "Oh said the Able Sea Bear, "I wonder what you are? I'd better stop and let you all off somewhere nice." With that he steered *The Little Blue Boat* to the river's edge and held onto the bank. He then carefully lifted the plants off the shrouds and laid them on the bank by some grass and reed.

"That," said a heron watching like a statue next to

him. "That is a very good thing to do. Those are the babies of a very, very rare creature."

"Oh what creature is that then?" asked Teddy.

"The Swallowtail butterfly," replied the heron motionless, apart from his beak, "they're the biggest native butterfly in this country and this is about the only place they live now."

"Oh," said Teddy looking carefully at the wriggling caterpillar-like creatures.

"It's because of what they're on, that's milk parsley," said the heron, "it's what they eat when they're young and this is about the only place it grows. You've done them a great favour, that idiot going too fast had torn the plant away and taken those babies with it. They'd have all died had it not been for you. Well done little bear."

"Er, it was nothing," smiled Teddy nervously. He asked the heron for a favour: "I'm not really strong enough to raise this mast, any chance you could help?" he asked nicely.

"I'll try but I might need a friend," replied the heron and called out. Another large bird joined him, and together they took the forestay - that's the piece of wire that holds up the mast at the front of the boat - and they pulled. The mast rose up and soon reached its full height. The Able Sea Bear tied the forestay off and clicked the boom into place. Thanking the herons, he pulled up the jib sail, as there was wind coming from behind them; it meant they could sail along using just the small front sail alone.

Soon they were being blown along the River Bure. "A sign," said Teddy, as he spotted a green direction sing pointing off to port (that's left, of course, in boat language). "Ranworth, OK let's try Ranworth," he said and off they went.

By the time they got to Ranworth the jib sail had been taken down and the little electric motor started. It was then, that Teddy saw something that made him very sad. The main sail, still tied around the boom, had a rip in it, a large rip. It had caught on something in Pincher Pete's mad race along the river. "Oh no!" said Teddy sadly, "How am I going to mend that? I'll have to stop for a ponder." So he stopped the small yacht in the reeds close to Ranworth Broad.

He tied the boat safely to an overhanging branch and tucked her well away into the reeds. He was very tired from all the worry, the panic and the events of the day. He sat down for a little snooze, hoping that an answer to his ripped sail problem would come to him in his sleep. It did.

Evening turned to night and night turned to morning and Teddy woke up to the sound of the main sail being hoisted up the mast.

W-what's going on?! He thought and rubbed his sleepy eyes with his paws. There was the mainsail hoisted up by two herons, their beaks holding the main halyard.

Flying around it, like bees around honey, were a mass of dragonflies, the famous Norfolk Hawker Dragonfly Display Team, known for their displays throughout the insect world. "Wow!" said the astounded Able Sea Bear.

"Wow indeed," said the heron, with the rope in his beak. "Look at your ripped sail!"

"Oh wow again!" said Teddy, delighted with what he saw. Crawling away down the main sail was an army of spiders. Together they'd used their web building skills to sew a patch on the ripped sail. It was made from an old piece tea towel that had blown off a boat. They found it, chewed it to shape and used their own silky thread to sew it on.

"Oh thank you, thank you!" said the Able Sea Bear in glee.

"They say it's a pleasure and thank you for what you did for the baby Swallowtails," said the heron, who then lowered the mended sail.

The spiders then crawled onto the backs of the herons, who flew them back to the reed beds where they lived. The dragonflies swooped, hovered and spun in the air, like ballerinas on a stage, their colours shining in the sun. Teddy was so pleased, and so was *The Little Blue Boat*.

Teddy felt more awake and more relaxed. He started the little electric motor and gently went into Malthouse Broad looking for the grandchildren. Lots of children were there, but not the ones he was looking for. Sadly he turned the boat around and headed out again. As he passed the entrance to Ranworth Broad he noticed some dark deep shapes under the water. "Oh, what are those?" he said to himself.

"Wherries, old sunken wherries," said a voice.

"Who's that?" asked the Able Sea Bear, and looking

up he saw a marsh harrier, the largest of the harriers and a famous bird of prey.

"The wherries are old trading boats. Long before railways and cars and lorries came along, people used the rivers to transport the things they bought and sold. In places like this it was the easiest and most direct way to transport things," continued the harrier, circling gracefully around the top of the mast,

"wherries were trading barges that went from place to place carrying everything from grain to coal, animals to reeds. As the railways and roads took over though, many turned to carrying people for pleasure but most owners had to scrap them in the end. Many of them were sunk in places like this to help shore up and protect the river banks. They are also home to the eels."

"The eels?" asked Teddy.

"Long, thin fish that live in families and slither and

slide around together, deep under the water. They look a bit like little snakes. They love old wrecks to swim and play in. People used to eat lots of them in the olden days but they're not so popular today. You can't take the boat inside Ranworth Broad because it's a Reserve, but if you want to see the sunken wherries more easily I'll take you over the top of the surface if you like: as the water's clear and you might see them."

Teddy climbed on the marsh harrier's back, and held on tight. The big bird flapped its wings and the wind whooshed by the Bear's ears as it took off. The harrier swooped just above the water and there below the surface the bear could see the outline of an old Wherry, its hull just a skeleton of what it used to be. He could just make out the bottom and lots of slithering creatures, the Eels, going between the wooden struts and bits of planking slowly rotting under the water.

"Wow!" said the Able Sea Bear, "any chance I could have a quick look for the grandchildren while I'm up here?" he asked.

"Of course," replied the bird and flew him over Ranworth Staithe where families had gathered to enjoy their day by the Information Centre.

They soared higher and higher, the river twisted and turned below them and vast areas of wonderful wetland were visible to the Able Sea Bear who was having a bird's eye view.

Sadly he couldn't tell which children where which as they all looked so small at that height. Then the marsh harrier took Teddy to the top of the highest nearby building, Ranworth Church Tower. The bird landed on the top of the tower and Teddy carefully got off its back and stood very carefully on the edge looking, at the amazing view.

"Ohh," said the Able Sea Bear, "that IS a long way down, but what a great view!"

People could be heard coming up the steps inside the top of the tower, the church attracts a lot of visitors who like to climb up and see for themselves.

The marsh harrier didn't want to alarm them so he asked Teddy to climb back on, and he took off, flying him back to *The Little Blue Boat*.

"DAD!" shouted a small boy who saw them. "There's a flying teddy bear!"

"Don't be silly," replied the boy's dad, helping someone up through the hatchway onto the tower, "bear's don't fly." But the boy knew better.

"Thank you, that was great!" said Teddy as he was landed back in the cockpit of *The Little Blue Boat*.

"No problem," replied the bird and took off.

Where next? thought the Able Sea Bear. *Perhaps Horning or Coltishall is where I'll find the grandchildren, come on Boat we can't give up now.*

The Able Sea Bear pulled up the sails and they set off, the new patch proudly on display as the old sails filled once more with wind.

CHAPTER SIX

The Ancient Burrows

The Little Blue Boat and its skipper, Able Sea Bear, Teddy, were heading towards Wroxham, where many visitors to the Broads begin their holidays or take boats out for a day. They'd left Ranworth and re-joined the River Bure. They did have a small problem though, the mast was up, and Teddy wasn't strong enough to lower it on his own. The mast would have to be lowered to allow them to get under Wroxham Bridge. Teddy was just wondering what to do when he saw the Marsh Man standing by the side of a small staithe. He was waving his old paddle gently to attract Teddy's attention. The Able Sea Bear turned the boat head to wind and lowered the sails. He then started the small electric motor and went alongside to talk to the friendly and mysterious man from the marshes.

"Hello," said the Marsh Man, grabbing hold of the mooring ropes and tying *The Little Blue Boat* up to the wooden posts, holding it firmly against the shore.

"Hello," said Teddy, who still found it strange that a human could understand him.

"I hear you've had a few adventures," said the Marsh Man, "not least with that criminal, Pincher Pete."

"Yes," replied the Able Sea Bear, "thankfully we're all OK."

"Would you like me to lower the mast for you so you can go under Wroxham Bridge and on to Coltishall to try and find these children you're looking for?"

"Oh yes please," said Teddy eagerly.

With that the Marsh Man undid the boom, took down the mast and carefully tied up the sails.

"Now then, I wonder if you might do us a little favour, well it's for the otters really."

"Of course, of course," said Teddy, "how can we help?"

"When you get to Coltishall, you will see a sign that says 'End of Navigation'; that means boats have run out of river that is deep enough or wide enough for them to continue their journey; or that there's a very low bridge ahead that doesn't open. Well when you get there, just go a little bit further, and wait for me. Shall I take that horrible, old, broken, petrol outboard away? I can take it to be recycled if you'd like?"

"Oh yes please," said the Able Sea Bear nodding. The Marsh Man undid the clips and lifted the old outboard off the back of *The Little Blue Boat*. It had been a fantastic engine in its day, but now it was old technology, and the electric outboard was better for the environment.

"Now off you go," said the Marsh Man, laying the old engine down for a moment while he untied the small yacht's mooring ropes.

"OK," said the puzzled bear. He started the electric

motor, and the Marsh Man pushed the boat off from the quay to help it on its way.

Soon the boat and the Able Sea Bear went through Horning, and then Wroxham with its bustle and happy holiday atmosphere. Wroxham Bridge is another low bridge, with a pilot for boats who need a bit of help getting under it. Teddy headed straight for the middle of the channel and, after checking the height of the water on the board at the side of the bridge, carefully steered the small yacht under the brickwork and out the other side. Nobody noticed there was a teddy bear at the tiller; everyone was too busy feeding the swans, eating ice creams or queuing for fish and chips by the bridge.

After a while *The Little Blue Boat* was in open water. The Able Sea Bear motored to the river bank and stopped. He recognised the herons who'd helped him before. "I say," he called out, "is there any chance you could help me raised the mast again? I'd love to sail."

The herons nodded their heads and flew over, grabbing the fore stay in their beaks, and, as the Able Sea Bear guided the mast, the two birds pulled it up. Teddy then attached the boom, and within minutes he was on his way, the gentle wind filling *The little Blue Boat's* sails.

Soon the river narrowed a little and they reached the village of Belaugh. Then a loud, noisy holiday cruiser came up behind them with young men on board who were shouting for *The Little Blue Boat* to get out of the way.

Well I'm not taking up much of the river, thought Teddy, and then added, *I bet they've been drinking.* Sure enough the cruiser went by with music blaring out. The young man at the wheel had a cheap pirate hat on and was swerving the boat from side to side; they were going so fast they made a lot of wash which hit the banks with a *splash*.

Suddenly as they went round a bend, Teddy saw a pair of great crested grebes; lovely birds who live on the water. They were in a real panic, swimming this way and that. The Able Sea Bear slowed the boat down to ask the mother grebe what the problem was, but he soon saw it for himself. The wash from the drunks' boat had washed three baby grebes out of their nest and they were too young to swim on their own.

The parents were in a real state. "Hold on!" shouted Teddy, "we'll help!" And he threw the boat's life ring into the water by the baby birds.

The young grebes looked towards their mother who shouted, "swim inside the ring, swim into it!" The babies did just that and the life ring protected them from the waves.

Soon the parents had gathered their babies and taken them back to the nest. Baby grebes travel on their mum and dad's backs when they're very young, and their nests float on the water in, or by reeds so they are very vulnerable to wash, which is one reason why there's a speed limit. The faster boats go, the more wash they make.

The Able Sea Bear put The Little Blue Boat back on

course, but soon found a further casualty of the drunken cruiser's antics. Another holiday boat was at the side of the river held by its mud weight - that's a sort of anchor often used in rivers, Broads and lakes. One of the people on board was holding a wet towel over their arm and they were crying. The other person was on their mobile phone. Teddy could hear what they were saying. "Hello, is that the Wroxham Health Centre? We need to find a nurse or a doctor, a cruiser went by us so fast, the wash it made knocked a saucepan of boiling water over my friend's arm, and it's *really* painful."

"Oh that's awful," said Teddy as he motored passed. Then he saw another result of too much drinking on the water. At the side of the long quayside at Coltishall by the lovely village green, the cruiser that had caused the trouble was tied up, but tied up very badly. A group of people were crouched over a young man who was lying on his back on the grass. His friends were all looking very worried. They'd tied up the boat and as they got off, he was so drunk he'd fallen between the boat and the Quayside and was unable to climb out of the river because he'd been drinking too much. It's very difficult at the best of times to climb out of the water, let alone if you're drunk.

The water was very cold even though it was summer and the boy had very nearly drowned. If a passing nurse hadn't turned up by chance he may well have died.

"Let that be a lesson," said the Bear under his breath as they went by.

"Well no sign of the grandchildren here, and this is the end of navigation, the furthest point up the River Bure we can get," said Teddy. Then he remembered the Marsh Man's meeting, so he crept right up to the 'End of Navigation' sign and stopped by a small piece of hard river bank. On it stood the Marsh Man.

"Hello Able Sea Bear," he said smiling, holding his paddle.

"Hello," replied Teddy, still puzzled as to why he'd been asked to come here.

"We need some help, there's a family of otters who moved, many, many years ago up the Bure to the farthest places, to the quietest of dykes to live in exile."

"Exile?" said Teddy even more puzzled.

"Yes exile, that's when you have to leave your homes," said the Marsh Man.

"Well they can now return. Years ago the place where they lived was so polluted by chemicals and sewage, yes that's right sewage, a whole town's sewage used to get pumped into the river. Well it was so bad that the Otters all had breathing problems, it was a bit like asthma, and they started to die. They couldn't live there any longer and they had to leave. It was every sad as they'd lived there for many generations and loved it. But they had to go. Now thanks to new rules from Europe and lots of helpful people who love the Broads, the pollution has been cleaned up, and the days of the 'Great Sludge', as it was known, are over. Now they can all go back and take over the old burrows where they used to live."

"That's lovely," said the Able Sea Bear, "but they swim don't they?"

"Yes they do swim," said the Marsh Man, "but they don't all know the way, and we need a distraction in case anyone sees masses of otters in the water together; they need an escort to help them get there safely, and they've got some luggage too," smiled the Marsh Man.

"We can do that, but if any humans stop us I can't talk to them," said Teddy anxiously.

"No, but I can, I'm coming with you, move over!" And with that, the Marsh Man got into *The Little Blue Boat*.

They were going to wait until nightfall before making the first part of the journey, as it would be easier to hide the otters when going through Wroxham and Horning. Otters are shy creatures that prefer moving about at night. They had been gathering and waiting for their journey on a stretch of river beyond Coltishall, where the water runs through ancient meadows and farmland. No one noticed them swim quietly under Horstead Road Bridge, and then clamber out of the water to scurry past the weirs that blocked the river.

The Little Blue Boat didn't have any navigation lights, but the Marsh Man had thought of that. As night fell, two fireflies buzzed out of the reeds and sat three quarters of the way up the mast. "That's your steaming light!" smiled the Marsh Man. Two more landed on the stern, "and there's your white light at the back that you are supposed to have." Two more fireflies landed on the port shroud and two on the starboard shroud.

"Shouldn't they be red for port, and green for starboard though, and not white?" asked the Able Sea Bear.

"Of course, and that's why I've cut up an old pair of 3D cinema glasses, which are red and green," grinned the Marsh Man. The fire flies danced behind the coloured plastic and sure enough *The Little Blue Boat* was up to standard, ready to navigate at night. Being a private boat *The Little Blue Boat* is allowed to travel at night on the Broads. Hire boats aren't allowed to of course.

The moon came up. The two pubs at Coltishall were full of happy holiday makers and people from the villages having a lovely evening. *The Little Blue Boat* gently moved off followed by ten families of otters, some old, some young and some expecting babies, babies who would be born where their ancestors were born many years ago.

Under a full moon the convoy went almost silently along the River Bure, passing sleepy boats and shut up houses, curtains closed against the night.

They decided to stop at Horning Church Staithe where the Marsh Man had lowered the mast the day before. They would do the rest of the journey in the morning as they'd now got through the busiest places on their route, and the river was wider. They'd travel the next day to St Benet's Abbey, then wait for nightfall again before travelling the last section up to Barton Broad.

The otters went fishing for their supper, and the

Marsh Man patted the Able Sea Bear on his head and told him he'd be back in the morning. The Boat and Teddy slept well, despite the noise of the youngest otters who were too excited to rest.

The next day the otters were waiting and the Marsh Man arrived, but so did someone else. It was the Bishop of Norwich. He walked down the path to the staithe and spoke to the Marsh Man. "Hello, I don't suppose you could give me a lift could you, you see as Bishop of Norwich I am also Abbot of St Benet's Abbey, it's a sort of honorary title as the Abbey is just a ruin now, but I like to go there from time to time. I was due to meet someone here to take me but they've been delayed."

"Of course Bishop do get in, excuse the teddy bear," smiled the Marsh Man who winked at Teddy. As the Bishop and Marsh Man chatted, Teddy looked round to see all the otters swimming behind, but when the Bishop looked round, the otters all ducked at once, and all he saw was rippling water.

The Bishop told the Marsh Man all about the abbey. The Marsh Man knew far more about it than the Bishop did, but he was very polite and listened anyway, as he was keen for the Able Sea Bear to hear the story.

"Way back in the Middle Ages," said the Bishop, "it was a very important monastery, that's where religious people called monks lived. It was very wealthy and had property in more than 75 villages. Like all old places it had good and bad times, and it's a very special place."

The Bishop carried on and Teddy listened intently.

"Only part of the old gatehouse and a wind pump

inside it are still standing today, but the abbey once covered a very large area. Archaeologists have found out where the monks built fish ponds to keep a supply of fresh fish to eat, but I don't think they had any chips!" laughed the Bishop. Teddy wanted to make a joke about there being 'chip-monks' but he thought better of it.

Soon they reached the abbey and the Marsh Man tied the boat up. The Bishop got out and thanked him; he looked round, and as he did all the otters dipped their heads under the water so as not to be seen. Everyone else who was moored up there was looking at the Bishop. It's not every day you see a Bishop get off a boat.

Most of the holidaymakers moored alongside the old abbey ground had no idea of how vast or important this place used to be. The Bishop knew, and could imagine how hard the life of the monks must have been; they had no modern comforts and lived very simple lives.

The Marsh Man untied the ropes again and they set off up the River Ant next to the abbey. The River Ant is narrower than the River Bure, and it twists and turns as it heads north. Soon they reached How Hill.

"How something, How something!" cried Teddy out loud. "*That's* where the grandchildren like walking!"

"Oh," replied the Marsh Man, "let's have a look." The Marsh Man tied up the small yacht, picked up Teddy and together they walked across to Toad Hall Cottage, which is now a lovely museum of how Broad's people used to live in the olden days.

The staff there hadn't seen the grandchildren, so the pair moved on. They walked the pretty path to the bird hide, a special wooden building where people can watch an amazing variety of birds on the water without upsetting or disturbing them. They searched the walks and the river banks, but there was no sign of the grandchildren that Teddy so desperately wanted to find.

Back in *The Little Blue Boat,* under the power of the electric motor, its battery charged by the solar panel soaking up the sunlight, they continued their journey, with the otters swimming behind. Soon they reached a bend in the river and the Marsh Man stopped the boat. The otters squeaked out loud and splashed and swam and went bonkers with happiness.

"This is where our great, great grannies lived!" said one youngster.

"I've seen drawings; they drew maps in the mud to show us," said another.

"Oh I know where we can find their old burrows; we can dig them out and move straight in!" said an older otter, sampling the water and sniffing the exciting air. The otters were so very happy.

"As it's a full moon tonight," said the Marsh Man, "there's a meeting of the Bittern Council, and you, you are invited."

"Oh no, no it's fine, it's OK, and er, I couldn't do that," stuttered Teddy, who was very shy at the best of times.

"Sorry Able Sea Bear, but if you're invited to attend the Bittern Council, you attend the Bittern Council," said the Marsh Man, looking taller and quite scary.

"OK," gulped Teddy.

"I'll show you where it is, I'll come with you, but you must never tell or show anyone else, for this is the secret of the Broads," said the Marsh Man sternly,

"No," gulped the bear again, "I won't tell, I really won't!"

They waited until dusk. The Marsh Man turned the boat and headed towards a reed-filled riverbank. *The Little Blue Boat* was worried she might be rammed into the riverbank, and the Able Sea Bear grabbed the sides, waiting for a collision; but it never came.

The reeds gave way; they were floating reeds, known as 'a hover', a large patch of floating reeds that were blocking the entrance to a small dyke.

The Little Blue Boat, Teddy and the Marsh Man went down into the dyke and the 'hover' moved back behind them, closing the entrance once again. Only the Marsh Man knew this entrance and he never told. They were heading for the Secret Broad, and the Bittern Council.

CHAPTER SEVEN

Arrested!

The moon was rising, gently bathing the sky with its deep yellow glow. *The Little Blue Boat* moved gently along the hidden dyke of which no human knows, except the Marsh Man, and he never tells.

The reeds touched the sides of the small yacht and the overhanging branches brushed her mast as they made their way. There was just enough water under her keel for them to avoid being grounded on the mud below; at times the boat would slow and then move again as the soft mud was pushed aside by her small twin keels – a keel is boat language for the part underneath a boat which sticks down under the water and stops yachts from going over in the wind and waves. There are different types of keel, *The Little Blue Boat* had two short stubby ones, one on each side of the centre of her hull, and it meant that she could go in very shallow water.

Soon the small dyke split into two. "Always take the left path," said the Marsh Man.

"But the other one looks bigger," replied the Able Sea Bear.

"The obvious path isn't always the best one to take,

and it's the smaller path here that leads to our destination."

The boat turned down the smaller path and, as she did, eyes watched from the reeds and branches. Big eyes: the owls were watching. Bats flew around and under watchful eye of the moon they reached the end of the small dyke. The Marsh Man had lowered her mast so she could squeeze under the overhanging branches and low trees along the route.

The entrance to the Secret Broad was suddenly lit by fireflies sitting on lily pads in a long line on the surface of the dark water. At the end of this line of lights was a branch of a fallen tree. Six birds sat motionless, their heads almost hidden and held low. Slowly they began to make their famous call, a low booming noise.

"Is it safe?" asked Teddy, shaking.

The Marsh Man held the frightened Able Sea Bear's soft paw. "Of course, this is the Bittern Council, the highest and wisest authority on the Broads. It's been that way since the Great Estuary."

"What was that?" asked Teddy intrigued.

"Oh," said the Marsh Man, "the landscape and the boundaries between the sea and the shore have changed a lot over thousands of years. When the Romans came here nearly 2,000 years ago, the town of Great Yarmouth, where you came in from the sea, wasn't there; that land was mostly underwater, just sandbanks. Lots of the land around there was under water and the rivers were wider. Slowly the movement of the tides and the flow of the rivers led to the changes, so the shoreline went further out towards where it is now, and the rivers became narrower.

"Is that how the Broads were formed?" asked Teddy.

"No," replied the Marsh Man, as the bittern's booming got louder. "Breydon Water near Yarmouth is part of what remains of the Great Estuary, but the Broads were formed in a different way, by people.

After the Romans, the Vikings came. Many people from Europe came and made their homes here. By the twelfth century most of the woodland that covered the ground had been chopped down for house building and for burning on fires to keep warm. People then looked to burn peat, that's lumps of boggy turf which when 'dried out' burns very well. It's very dense you see and made up of lots of compressed bits of leaf and wood and stems and things like that, and it can keep fires going for a long time in cold winters. They used fires to cook on then as well, because there was no gas or electricity or oil, and no one had ovens and cookers like people do today. "

"So what happened next?" asked Teddy.

"Well, when you dig a hole around here, which they did when they dug out the peat, it fills up with water. You can tell they dug the Broads because the sides of the Broads are straight down, and the sides of natural lakes are sloping. So that's how we know that man made them. We also know this because the birds and animals have passed the story down through countless generations."

"Oh," said the Able Sea Bear.

"Sadly, a long time ago the people just took everything they could from the Broads; they killed lots of birds and animals without thinking of the consequences."

"Consequences?" asked Teddy.

"Consequences means what happens as a result of what you do," smiled the Marsh Man. "Take the bitterns, there are now only a few of them left, because they were slow, noisy and to some people they tasted nice. So people killed them, nearly all of them. Luckily they are protected now but it was only just in time. We nearly lost them forever, like the otters who were forced out by the Great Sludge when man polluted the Broads and rivers, and made the otters homes impossible to live in." The Marsh Man was quite angry. Telling Teddy these things made him sad and cross to think what people had done to the environment that he loved so much.

"Would it be better if the people left and went away then?" asked Teddy.

"No," said the Marsh Man, "man made the Broads so man must maintain them, and the people who love the Broads are now in charge and making sure they are protected. Now, hush, the Bittern Council is about to start!"

The Marsh Man and Teddy sat quietly in *The Little Blue Boat*. They were part of a big audience, almost every type of bird and animal were represented. Birds and animals that sometimes ate each or squabbled over territory had put aside their differences and had a truce, on the orders of the Bittern Council.

The booming got louder and sounded like drumming. Then the rhythm changed and the booms got shorter and faster.

"The bitterns' boom is like the heartbeat of the Broads!" said the excited Able Sea Bear.

"Shhh," said the Marsh Man.

The bitterns raised their heads and looked around. An owl blinked its big eyes and said, "The Council is now in session, you will all respect the bitterns."

Then, the largest bittern in the centre of the log, spoke.

"Gathering, we have an apology from the little terns; they are too busy with their chicks to send anyone tonight. We first need to discuss a few issues regarding the cormorants." The bittern paused and looked around. Then, clearing her throat she spoke again. "Step forward please."

"Who's that?" asked Teddy in a whisper.

"She," replied the Marsh Man quietly, "Is the Bittern Empress."

Then a big dark cormorant waddled up before the Council. Cormorants are large dark seabirds which are easily recognisable as they stand on posts in the water to dry their wings. It was this, which was causing a few problems.

"We know," said the bittern, "that you like and you need to dry your wings out on posts, but please, leave a few posts for other birds to stop on. You are hogging them a little; you can't just sit there all day you know. Please tell your family and friends to move on when other birds need to stop for a rest. It's like a few people

who fish from quaysides and who won't move when boats need to moor there. You are very welcome to use the posts but please move on gracefully when others need to use them," said the Bittern Empress.

The Able Sea Bear and the Marsh Man listened as a range of issues were discussed. The bitterns then turned to something else. "The otters," said a bittern on the end of the branch. "We notice they've now moved back to the Ancient Burrows which were deserted due to the Great Sludge. This is very good news and great thanks must be given to *The Little Blue Boat* and it's Able Sea Bear who helped make this happen."

The birds and animals shook wings, clattered beaks and clapped paws in appreciation. The otters jumped out of the water and twisted and turned in delight. The Able Sea Bear was very shy and very embarrassed to be the centre of attention.

"That brings us to the other issue, that of theft and a certain character who we all know. It is the duty of ALL who live on, above, in, or who visit the Broads to combat crime wherever we see it. By crime I mean theft and vandalism and also littering. We had three young swans in terrible pain after swallowing discarded fishing line, and two baby ducks died after getting their heads cut by rusting tins that had been thrown away into the reeds. If we can't deal with it ourselves we must try to make the rangers aware. There are only a few problem people, but a few can make a big difference. I hear some teenage boys untied the mooring ropes of a holiday cruiser which was then carried by the tide and hit a bridge. People can easily get hurt," said the bittern sternly, "holiday makers don't always realise the power of the tides, and stupid behaviour must be stopped whenever we see it."

The Council continued for much of the night before closing, as it always did, with stories of the past and some soft singing in the moonlight by a pair of Nightingales.

The Marsh Man turned *The Little Blue Boat* around and headed back out along the dyke. Dawn was approaching. As they reached the end of the dyke the "hover" - the floating reeds which blocked the exit -

moved to the side, and the small yacht re-joined the River Ant. The "hover" closed behind them and the entrance to the dyke was hidden once more.

A few minutes later they arrived at Irstead Staithe. "I'm getting off here," said the Marsh Man, "But I'll raise your mast and sails for you so you can sail up to the End of Navigation on this river, just passed Wayford Bridge. I'll be there to drop the mast for you again." With that, he raised the small yacht's mast and, holding the boat head to wind at an angle to the quay, he helped the Able Sea Bear set the sails.

As the small yacht sailed gently up the River Ant, the wide expanse of Barton Broad came in to view. Teddy steered *The Little Blue Boat* around the small island, and across the open water. "I'm sure the grandchildren come somewhere near this Broad," said Teddy, "I'm sure I remember Rod, the boat's owner, mentioning its name." With that they sailed on up the river towards Wayford Bridge, passing the turning for Stalham and the lovely Museum of the Broads on their way.

After they passed the boatyards they saw the Marsh Man waiting on the bank just before Wayford Bridge where he promised he would be. He grabbed their ropes and tied the boat safely to the shore. Then, true to his word, he lowered the mast again. "Your battery is probably charged up now from the solar panel, so your little electric outboard will work again," he said.

"Thank you," said Teddy, and they waved goodbye. The motor started and the small yacht went under Wayford Bridge.

Passing a row of holiday houseboats, the Able Sea Bear said, "OK Boat, let's go to the right, oh sorry, the Starboard side; it looks like an interesting little stream."

The stream was interesting but it got narrower and narrower and the water got shallower and shallower. A canoe passed by but there were no other vessels on this stretch of water.

Soon they came to Tonnage Bridge. "Wow" said Teddy, "that's it, we're at the very End of Navigation, even for this small yacht. That bridge is very low." Then as he turned, *The Little Blue Boat* got stuck. The water was too shallow even for her short twin keels. "Oh no," said the Able Sea Bear, "I've broken a rule of good seamanship and run aground!" It wasn't always like this, what they were on used to be a canal which joined the Broads and rivers with the town of North Walsham. Here, small wherries would take goods and supplies up and down before the roads and railways took over.

Luckily for Teddy it was a just a lump of mud under the water, and with a bit of pulling and pushing on the tiller, and with the small motor on full power, they were free. "There are no grandchildren here, but it is a beautiful place. Let's stop here for the night," Said Teddy, so he tied the small yacht to an old tree branch, turned off the electric motor and fell into a deep sleep.

The next morning they set off again. They re-joined the main river and took the other turn in the River Ant and went towards Dilham, in the hope that the grandchildren might just be there. Soon they were coming to the End of Navigation on this branch of the river, and they could see a turning area ahead.

They also saw something else: a dark, shadowy figure climbing out of the kitchen window of one of the houses whose gardens backed onto the river.

"That's Pincher Pete!" said Teddy, "Let's run!" Then he stopped and thought, *No we must catch him; if he gets away he'll always be a menace. It's dangerous I know, but we must let ourselves be stolen by him and try to raise the alarm somehow.* Was the Able Sea Bear being very brave, or very stupid?

Teddy steered *The Little Blue Boat* onto the river bank along the bottom of the garden of the house that Pincher Pete had just robbed. A neighbour had seen the thief and was shouting at him. The burglar looked around for someway of escape, the road would be useless as the neighbour could run after him, then he saw *The Little Blue Boat*. "I can't believe my luck!" he sneered. "I can nick that dam boat again and this time it'll be my get-away car, or er... get-away boat, ha ha!"

He ran down to the river bank and threw a bag of stolen stuff into the cabin. There was a clock given to the owner as a present, a laptop computer and a painting of two yachts. Before he made his escape he undid the ropes on two other moored boats so they would float away and block the river to make sure that no one could follow him. "Ha ha!" he said as he started the little electric motor and headed off as fast as he could make it go.

The neighbour called the police and then stood at the side of the rive,r shouting after the horrible thief.

Pincher Pete saw the Able Sea Bear sitting motionless in the cockpit and kicked him into the cabin. "Ouch!" said Teddy, who landed by the compartment that stored the battery for the motor. He made sure Pincher Pete was looking ahead and then put his paw inside the little opening; he undid the wire from the battery to the motor just at the right time. The power was turned off, so the motor stopped, and the boat just started drifting towards the end of the row of houseboats near Wayford Bridge, right next to where the Broads Beat Police Land Rover had just pulled up. The neighbour had raised the alarm and the police knew there was only one way Pincher Pete could go, so they were waiting for him.

Pincher Pete turned the tiller and said, "I'll pull up the sails, oh I can't the mast is down and there's Wayford Bridge ahead! Blast, I'll have to leap off and leg it." Then the rangers' launch came under the bridge, they'd been alerted too. Pincher Pete said, "I know, I'll lie down low so no one can see me, I can paddle under the bridge and then escape through the boat yards." Teddy heard him and had to make sure the police and the rangers knew that Pincher Pete was on-board.

Pincher Pete threw himself into the little cabin right by Teddy. He rolled over and there in front of the Able Sea Bear's mouth, was Pincher Pete's rather unpleasant bottom. Teddy knew he had to make sure the rangers and the police could find Pincher Pete, so he did what he'd never done before and, holding his breath, he bit hard. He bit right through Pincher Pete's shabby old trousers and pants, and sank his teeth into the horrible thief's bum!

"Agh, ooh, oww!"shouted Pincher Pete, who leapt up, banged his head on the roof of the cabin, then rushed out into the cockpit and promptly knocked himself out on the boom. Teddy kept quiet.

The Little Blue Boat drifted into the bank right next to the police car. "You're under arrest!" shouted the police officer and rushed towards the boat. The ranger brought his patrol boat alongside *The Little Blue Boat*, and grabbed Pincher Pete's arms, just as the policeman slapped handcuffs on his wrists.

"There's a nice cell waiting for you Pincher Pete," said the police officer.

"Good job we caught him," said the ranger.

All Pincher Pete could say was "I've been bitten on the bum, by a teddy bear!"

"He must have hit his head harder than we thought, he's imagining things," said the policeman.

As Pincher Pete was led away he couldn't believe his eyes, he could see through the tiny window on the small yacht, and there in the cabin looking out was a teddy bear waving goodbye. "I WAS bitten by a teddy bear, he's a dangerous wild animal!" he said, as the police Land Rover drove off with its blue light flashing.

The ranger tied up *The Little Blue Boat* and then went to help tie up the boats which Pincher Pete had untied in Dilham. An otter poked her head up beside the small yacht. "Are you OK Teddy?" she asked.

"Oh yes," replied Teddy, climbing out of the cabin and getting back into the cockpit, "I wouldn't mind cleaning my teeth though."

"Look, you need to move now. The entire otter population and all the birds have been scouring the Broads for the grandchildren, and we think we've found them; they're on the boardwalk at the end of Barton Broad. Come on, there's no time to lose!"

With that, the Able Sea Bear untied the mooring ropes while no one was looking, then reconnected the small electric motor. Sadly the battery was almost flat, nearly all the power had been used up by Pincher Pete running it flat out. There was just enough to get under Wayford Bridge and then the motor stopped.

Teddy scratched his head, then, the 'not that common cranes flew down from the top of the bridge. They were joined by two herons and a rather scruffy goose, but between them they pulled up *The Little Blue Boat's* mast.

"Come on, come on," said the otter swimming behind, "there's no time to lose! No time at all!"

CHAPTER EIGHT

"No Time to Lose!"

There was no time to lose. Able Sea Bear, Teddy held the tiller firmly in his paws.

"Hurry, there's simply no time to lose," bubbled the eldest otter, rising out of the water.

"I know, I know," spluttered the Able Sea Bear, "but it's not easy. I'll hoist the sails, but there's hardly a breath of wind."

"But if the grandchildren go without seeing you, they might never return!" replied the otter, who dived back under the water.

The River Ant moved very gently, it's low, soft sides merging into water meadow and woodland as they past. On the edge of the river stood the Marsh Man, his old gnarled hand firmly holding an ancient paddle, its chestnut-brown wood blackened by the years. He nodded, smiled a little, and then looked to the trees.

"Oh this IS hopeless," said Teddy. "Come on little blue boat do try to help!"

The Little Blue Boat seemed to almost waggle her tiller to help the rudder move water from side to side;

any extra few centimetres would help shorten their journey. They'd come so far, surely they couldn't fail now? Then to make matters worse, a large cloud lay ahead. "Oh not again!" said Teddy, who was really beginning to get cross and lose his sense of humour. "Not mosquitoes!" Even Teddies can be bitten by mossies. Yes, they had their place and every right to live on the rivers, *but please*, thought Teddy, *don't come looking for a Bear to nibble at right now!*

The mosquito cloud got closer and thicker as the boat came under the shadow of the trees. The familiar quiet buzzing noise, which can wake you from the nicest of dreams, got louder. Teddy put one paw over his head to wave them away as they sized him up as a snack. The tree cover quickly cleared and, as the mosquitoes followed the boat they were exposed in the sun. Then from above the branches in the summer sky, some even hungrier creatures spotted them.

"YIPPEE" shouted Teddy, "Swallows!" and swooping down from an incredible height, a squadron of swallows soared and darted between the highest trees and the water, and that put the mossies into a real panic. Soon the nibbling pests had become food for the swooping swallows and those that could escape had gone back to the shadows.

The leaves suddenly began to shudder in the otherwise motionless trees. A noise, familiar and comforting, grew louder and louder, a whooshing sound, like bellows in great granny's fireplace. It was the swans! Two families, twelve swans in all, grown-ups and signets together, flapping their wings in unison were making a breeze.

"WOW!" shouted Teddy, "Come on Boat, we've got to make use of this!" And with that the Able Sea Bear waved his hands to ask the swans to pause and stop the draft so that he could raise the sails.

He let go of the tiller. "Hold yourself steady now Boat, I'm pulling up the sails!" And with that he hoisted the main sail, and then the jib.

"OK SWANS!" shrieked the Able Sea Bear "LET US HAVE ALL THE WING POWER YOU'VE GOT!"

The swans nodded their graceful heads on their steady long necks, and began beating their massive wings together like a Mexican wave. Holding themselves behind *The Little Blue Boat* they created a stiff breeze, and Teddy was soon in control. "Woooah *Little Blue Boat*, we've got the wind now!" And they certainly had.

The swans weren't alone though, and as they had to break formation and fly above the trees to avoid other boats, the otters helped below.

Under the water and back out again, breaking the surface, the beautifully sleek creatures with their webbed paws and strong muscular tails worked together, and pushed *The Little Blue Boat* along. Nothing could stop her now.

Other boats were surprised, and their crews were amazed. Here was *The Little Blue Boat* thundering along at a great rate of knots with no large outboard to be seen. Behind it was a rippling, gurgling mass of water, as if a huge engine were churning up the surface and breaking all the rules. Behind, and above there were teams of swans with their wings funnelling the air into a current which was being blown into the sails of *The Little Blue Boat*.

The boat, the otters, the Swans and Able Sea Bear Teddy, passed the turning for Stalham and were soon entering the beautiful Barton Broad.

"Nearly there, we're nearly there!" shouted the Able Sea Bear excitedly. *The Little Blue Boat* seemed to wag her tiller in agreement. Her sails were now picking up the natural wind across the Broad, which gave the swans and the otters the chance to have a rest. The escort service was by no means over though. The grebes started appearing at regular intervals along the route, rising out of the water in turn, each with a silver fish dancing in its beak, showing the way like lights on an airport runway. Their path led right across the water to the board walk at the end.

Ahead though, there was a race. It was the old wooden river cruisers. Big, heavy and strong, full of wind and out to play. Oddly though, they seemed to sense the urgency in *The Little Blue Boat* and to the amazement of those on board them, and to the other people watching, these graceful princesses of the rivers turned themselves to wind and stopped in their tracks, their sails luffing up and flapping. They were making sure *The Little Blue Boat* could pass by as quickly as she could. The word was out, this was a vital voyage, a journey so important, that it had even been discussed at the Bittern Council.

Their crews, though, were not always so helpful. Not knowing why their boats were misbehaving, helmsmen turned tillers and crews hauled in jib sheets, fighting to turn their vessels back, to pick up the wind and win the race. The boats fought their crews and their crews fought the boats, not knowing quite what they were doing wrong or why the boats were behaving as they were. A few collided with the painful sound of wood rubbing against wood, and sails tangling with booms and bowsprits.

The rescue boats roared into action; strong, rigid inflatables with powerful outboard motors, rushed into the chaos to help anyone who might fall overboard. These sailors were the best; they had years of experience of the wind, rain and storms in wild and distant places. They soon had their boats under control and no real damage was done. *The Little Blue Boat* had been allowed to pass through the race unhindered.

Soon the boardwalk was in sight, and there, pointing towards them, were the grandchildren and their father. Teddy saw them first and turned *The Little Blue Boat* head to wind and made her sails flap wildly.

The children and their father saw the commotion and recognised *The Little Blue Boat*. They rushed back along the boardwalk path, hoping to get onto the road and walk to Gays Staithe, which was the nearest place a boat could moor up.

As they did, Teddy, tiller firmly in his paws, turned *The Little Blue Boat* and found the wind. Passing the Nancy Oldfield Trust, which helps people with disabilities enjoy the water, they sailed between the old red and green wooden posts as the river narrowed. Suddenly the way was blocked; a cruiser was going very slowly across their path. Two boys were fishing from the back of the cruiser, long lines trailing out behind them.

"Oh no!" said the Able Sea Bear, "that's wrong, you should never fish from a moving boat, you never know what you might get tangle up in, and it's a real hazard to others." That wasn't all; everyone knows that boats should give way to sailing boats because with their sails up, they can only go where the wind will let them. "Oh," muttered Teddy in frustration, "please get out of our way, if I have to tack I'll lose the wind and lose all my speed."

Then, seeing the situation, a holidaymaker in a multi-coloured cruiser shouted to the fishing boat,

"Hey, have you seen that little blue boat coming? Please remember it's their right of way!"

With that the fishing boat's skipper gave a friendly wave back, the boys reeled in their fishing line and the cruiser increased its speed and motored to the side of the river, letting *The Little Blue Boat* pass by. Suddenly, Gays Staithe came into view.

There was another hazard ahead though, the journey wasn't over yet! "Oh no!" gasped Teddy. "There's nowhere to moor up!" It was the height of the holiday season and the holiday makers were making use of the moorings as they should. Brightly coloured cruisers sat side by side, fender to fender, whilst their crews and passengers relaxed in the soft, gentle sun.

Then, just as the Able Sea Bear was wondering what to do, a small boy on a cruiser shouted, "Dad DAD! Otters!" And everyone on Gays Staithe looked up. Yes, the otters had followed them, and, even though they are very shy and reserved creatures, the otters, desperate to help, started to put on a special show; a show like no holiday maker had ever seen before. Here were scores of otters swimming in formation catching fish, and twisting and turning in the water, like performing athletes. It was a fantastic display. They then moved off down the little cut towards Neatishead, and the holiday makers, fascinated and keen to see more, quickly switched on their engines, untied their cruisers and set off to follow them; it was almost like the Pied Piper.

Half-eaten picnics grabbed from table cloths on the grass, books and iPods hurriedly thrown below decks, and lifejackets quickly put on over crumpled tea shirts and tops. They'd never seen anything like this and they wanted to see all they could.

Soon the quay was empty, and Teddy and *The Little Blue Boat* gently drifted alongside the very end of the quay heading. With the sails down, Teddy grabbed the wooded edges where the river met the land, and rapidly tied the mooring lines, holding the vessel securely.

Then, the newly found silence was shattered, broken in the nicest way, by the sound of happy children. The grandchildren that our adventurers had fought so hard to find were actually there. They were delighted and very happy, but not nearly as happy as, Able Sea Bear, Teddy and *The Little Blue Boat*.

*

A month had passed by. The grey light of dawn slowly crept over the sleeping boats tied up snuggly in Cox's Boat Yard at Barton Turf.

The Little Blue Boat was sitting on a trailer. A snoozing Teddy woke with a yawn as a spider crawled over his nose. The boat had been pulled out of the water on a slipway and allowed to dry out for a few weeks.

During that month *The Little Blue Boat's* new owners, their dad and their friends, had cleaned her up, washed her down and repainted her hull with anti-foul; that's a special paint to stop shell-fish and plants growing on the undersides of boats. They'd only used the safest type though, anti-foul can be nasty stuff, and you have to make sure you put it on safely.

The Little Blue Boat's original owner, the children's granddad from Essex, was now out of hospital and recovering at home. He'd officially handed over the boat to the next generation, but only on the promise that the children continued taking sailing lessons and learned how to swim. This they'd done. Now cleaned and with her sails washed, *The Little Blue Boat* was ready once again for a life on the ocean waves. Well The Broads at least.

Today was a special day; the grandchildren, eleven year old Lucy, nine year old Sam and seven year old Alfie, were being allowed to sail on their own. Their dad would be right behind them in a fast canoe, ready to help at a moment's notice. It was also a race day, so the Safety Boats would soon be out on Barton Broad and ready to help.

With their new life-jackets firmly in place, the children pushed *The Little Blue Boat* down the slip way, into the water and climbed aboard. Able Sea Bear, Teddy was of course already sitting firmly in the cockpit. Unbeknown to the children, he'd been up most nights, cleaning crumbs and dusting the little cabin; re-housing spiders who were always creeping aboard, and fending off mosquitoes who were always skulking in the shadows.

The children used the paddles and headed out to Barton Broad. They turned the boat into the gentle wind so they could hoist the sails. They wanted to sail to Pleasure Hill Island, but the wind seemed to be dropping. Their father was behind them in his bright red canoe, life jacket on as always.

The clouds gathered from nowhere, filling the sky with shades of grey. Then, just as it looked like a storm was about to throw rain down on them, it suddenly cleared. As it did a gentle sound grew louder and louder, echoing across the water like the drum beat of a steady heart. "Boom, boom, boom." It wasn't just the sound of one, but of all six bitterns from the Bittern Council. "Boom, boom, boom".

Everything else went silent. Then suddenly, rising from the reeds like a torrent of water, came the marsh harriers; from beneath the waves popped up the otters, and then the grebes with small silver fish in their ever hungry beaks.

The "Brown Angles", the Norfolk Hawker Dragon-fly Display team, flitted across the surface of the water; they were followed by the Swallowtails flashing their colours in the sun. Other birds swooped across the reed-fringed shoreline, and water deer popped up their heads one by one. Standing between the deer in the reeds by the edge of the Broad, the Marsh Man appeared, waving his old wooden paddle. "Welcome home," he said softly, "welcome home to where you belong".

"Oh wow!" exclaimed Lucy, with a grin as big as a pancake.

"Corrr!" said Alfie, jumping up and down in the cockpit and rocking the boat. "What wonderful friends you have *Little Blue Boat* and Teddy. What adventures we're going to have together!" laughed Sam, pulling up the sails.

Yes, yes we are, said Teddy to himself, then he secretly saluted all of their friends.

The Marsh Man saluted back, unseen by anyone, except of course Able Sea Bear, Teddy, and *The Little Blue Boat*.

Animal and Bird Biographies

Swans

- The Swan in our story is a "mute" swan, which is often seen on our rivers.
- Mute Swans are white, very big, with a famous long, "S" shaped neck.
- Among Swans favourite foods are water plants, snails and insects.
- Swans can be grumpy, and may "hiss" at you if you get too close to their nests or their chicks, but they are only trying to protect them.
- Swans are the largest members of the duck and goose family.

Bitterns

- Bitterns are very hard to see because they are very shy and secretive, but their famous loud "booming" call can be heard a long way away.
- Bitterns look quite similar to herons with pale brownish coloured feathers.
- The best places to see Bitterns is by the edges of reed beds looking for fish.
- Bitterns' favourite food includes fish, amphibians and insects.
- Bitterns were once hunted for food and there are now just a few breeding pairs left in the UK.

Common Cranes

- Common Cranes can be found from Western Europe to Siberia.
- A pair of Common Cranes will build a nest in wetland areas out of vegetation.
- They are known to cover themselves in mud which might be for camouflage.
- These birds have long legs, a long neck and drooping, curved tail feathers.
- Their favourite foods are seeds, insects, worms and snails.

Otters

- Otters live along the edges of water, but are badly affected by pollution.
- Otters are considered to be quite clever and are friendly, but they can bite if they get worried or frightened.
- Otters spend most of their days in their homes and come out at night to find food.
- Otters were nearly wiped out in Britain due to people hunting and killing them and because of pollution, but they are now, slowly, returning.
- Otters favourite foods are mainly fish, but they will eat birds and frogs.

Norfolk Hawker Dragonfly

- This is a rare species. It has green eyes, clear wings and a yellow triangle on its body.
- Dragonflies flap their wings up to 30 times a second. Dragonflies can fly forwards, backwards and even sideways.

Norfolk Hawker Dragonflies like to live by slow flowing dykes and ditches

Their favourite foods are other insects.

Marsh Harrier

- The Marsh Harrier is the biggest of the harrier family.
- Marsh Harriers can fly very slowly, which allows them to spend longer flying over marshes, reeds and fens looking for food.
- These large birds of prey were quite rare a few decades ago, but thanks to wildlife conservation efforts in recent years, they've increased and are now thriving again.
- The female sits on eggs on the nest whilst the male finds food. When he does, he will call her, and as the female flies to meet him he will often drop the food for her to catch.
- The Marsh Harrier's favourite foods are frogs, small animals and small birds.

Pike

- The Pike is about the biggest and most fearsome fish in the inland waterways of Britain.
- Pike have very strong, powerful jaws, with a pointed head and sharp teeth.
- Pike live in slow flowing, fresh water streams, rivers, lakes and Broads.
- Pike ambush their prey by waiting, motionless in the water for food to come by. Then when close enough, they move very quickly, grabbing their prey sideways in their mouths.
- Pike's favourite foods are fish, but they will also eat baby ducklings and water voles.

Coming Soon!

Can the children save the bitterns eggs from Pincher Pete and an evil gang?

Will they stop an underwater war and an invading army of shellfish?

Will they get in trouble as they race through the Southern Rivers with gold treasure from an ancient Viking longboat?

What happens when they dare to sneak out to sea?

And, will the Marsh Man's true identity finally be revealed?

That's all in ***The Little Blue Boat and the Marsh Man's Gold!*** coming soon!